Does the River Ever End?

by Michael E. Owens

Trinity Press
Atlanta
Published by Scribblers Press
9741 SE 174th Place Road
Summerfield, FL 34491

Library of Congress
US Programs, Law, and Literature Division
Cataloging-in-Publication Program
101 Independence Avenue, S.E.
Washinton, DC 20540-4283
Library of Congress Contol Number: 2020906256

Owens, Michael E. 07/04/2020

Does The River Ever End? / Michael E. Owens This book is a work of
fiction. The characters, incidents, and dialogue are drawn from the author's
imagination and are not to be construed as real. Any resemblance to actual
events or persons, living or dead, is entirely coincidental.
ISBN 978-1-950308-13-2

Acknowledgments

I must thank my parents, Mary and Joe, first of all, for allowing me to spent time in my room writing as a pre-teen when most kids (at that time in history!) were outside, building forts and treehouses, riding bikes and constructing racers, playing with friends and staying out until the streetlights came on. Those many stories I wrote then are now long gone and lost forever in the rubble of my room. (My mother was a clean freak and nothing passed her eyes that didn't need to be tossed – and it was!)

It wasn't until high school did my writing get recognized. Competing against the best brains in my school of 1800 boys at East Jefferson High School in Metairie, Louisiana, I won the Gold Medal Award for Journalism in my senior year. Why I didn't pursue a career in writing as I enter college, I will never know.

In college, at Louisiana College, in Pineville, Louisiana, I was encouraged to continue writing by my history professor, Dr. Thomas Howell. He noted my writings for projects in his class and it gave me the feeling of pride and accomplishment and the germ to build on my writing skills.

As I began my career in the education field, I was responsible for writing many training manuals, instructional books, program plyers and other literature related to special education. Still I did not see me publishing any of the other personal writings with which I was involved.

It was not until my late wife Bonnie encouraged me to think about publishing my work did I begin to buckle down and get serious about it.

Not until my move from Louisiana to Georgia in 2015, and my subsequent retirement, did I find more time to write.

Then, my marriage to Leda the following year was the catalyst that prodded me to make my first novel a reality. With her great support, strong encouragement and sincere inspiration to believe in myself and follow my dream, I am publishing my first novel. She has been with me throughout the process of writing editing, reediting, meeting with publisher and artist, and attending my writer's group meetings every month. Her patience and understanding as I spent hours at the computer writing made my work much easier. I thank her for that. She was definitely my rock.

I also want to thank those closest to me who keep the faith going and were encouragers to me as well. First, my oldest granddaughter, Grace Crouch, read my book and offered her suggestions and corrections. I appreciate her interest in my work. And I give thanks to my children, Kristen Crouch, Kyle Owens and Kelly Owens, who allowed me to move from Baton Rouge and find a new life, find a new dream and to find a new wife. This freedom I found after my move to Georgia and the support of my kids and my grandkids gave me the hope and the future I felt God had allowed me to have.

I want to thank Woody Driskill, a fellow actor with the Phoenix Players, who also is a well-respected retired media specialist (a librarian as we knew them in the old days!) in several counties as well as the Georgia Department of Education. His encouragement was much relished.

Many thanks also to Charles de Andrade, the untiring leader and faithful organizer of the Scribblers'- a Christian writers' group. Our monthly meetings at the Crossing Restaurant in Norcross. Georgia were a not-to-be-missed event for anyone who is a serious published or a would-be published writer. His insightfulness and deep knowledge of the ins and outs of being published helped all of us. I was especially blessed to sit at the table with him and soak in his wisdom not only of the printing business but his understanding of Scripture and Biblical truths.

Of course, I would be remiss if I did not thank my editor, Casey Cox Daniels. I was amazed how much she truly delved into my book and asked the right questions that ultimately made my book a better read and a much-improved story. Her attention to detail surpassed my own knowledge of the words I put on paper. I became a better writer because of her.

And then I must thank my publisher, Trinity Press of Norcross, Georgia, who work feverishly to complete my book for the annual Decatur Book Festival, the largest book festival in the world. Joe Dye and his staff made the process seem so effortless. I want to especially thank Bridgett Joyce for her cover design, and the entire pre-press and press people who made this book possible.

Then there were the countless others whose prayers, encouragement, and inspiration was so vital to my desire to continue my writing journey.

Thanks to you all, and God bless you everyone!

Forward

Mike Owens is a true artisan. Not only does he write, but he also creates musicals, and acts in both his own and other works. As a Christian writer, one is often left thinking that writing needs to be spiritual in some way, but Mike finds wonder in the simple things in life, and demonstrates why everyday life should be wonderful to consider. Whether it is a series of poems about the reasons children might give for not liking vegetables, or the stories about cattle drives, and life in the west, or the life of a river boat man, and the trials of the son of the man known as Mike Fink, Mike Owens tells stories that you can visualize and relate to. For Mike, writing is about telling stories, and he does an exceptional job developing the characters and then connecting their lives with his readers. Enjoy his foray into published storytelling, it will be time well spent.

Charles de Andrade
Author
Steward Series
www.stewardseries.com

TABLE OF CONTENTS

PROLOGUE vi

CHAPTER 1 - The Captain 1

CHAPTER 2 - The Town...3

CHAPTER 3 - The Slave 5

CHAPTER 4 - The Request..9

CHAPTER 5 - Finding Out About Cletus.....................................13

CHAPTER 6 - Heading Home...19

CHAPTER 7 - Mrs. Bird 23

CHAPTER 8 - Supper That Night...27

CHAPTER 9 - Things Only Got Worse 31

CHAPTER 10 - Who Could Save Me Now? 37

CHAPTER 11 - Fugitives on the Run...41

CHAPTER 12 - Cletus Was Shot 47

CHAPTER 13 - Finding Food Wasn't Easy 53

CHAPTER 14 - An Unpleasant Encounter 57

CHAPTER 15 - The Cabin Was Not Empty 63

CHAPTER 16 - The Ohio 69

CHAPTER 17 - Finding a Way Down River 73

CHAPTER 18 - The Whole Truth 79

CHAPTER 19 - They Came After Blackwater 83

CHAPTER 20 - Heading Back Towards Cairo 89

CHAPTER 21 - Getting Past Cairo..95

CHAPTER 22 - Avoiding the Law..101

CHAPTER 23 - Everyone has a Question....................................105

CHAPTER 24 - Tales of the Mighty Mississippi..........................111

CHAPTER 25 - Storm on the River 115

CHAPTER 26 - Who Were These Men? 119

CHAPTER 27 - Cletus the Rescuer 121

CHAPTER 28 - The Storm was Over 125

CHAPTER 29 - Things Are Looking Up.....................................129

CHAPTER 30 - Trying to Get the Truth About Cletus.................133

CHAPTER 31 - Back to Normal on the River 139

CHAPTER 32 - A Lot of Explaining to do 143

CHAPTER 33 - A Surprising Reunion 147

PROLOGUE

"So, You're Mike Fink!"

I couldn't rightly recollect any time in my life that I did not have men stopping and staring at the mention of my name.

Often, I would hear them say, "Fink? Did I hear someone say Fink? Mike Fink?"

Other times, I would just see their reaction. First, they were taken aback. Then they would look me up and down from head to toe to head again, and then they would look me square in the eye. Their own eyes would squint as if studying my every facial and bodily feature.

There were probably many physical attributes about myself that favored my dad. Our eyes were dark and deeply set. Our hair was black as coal, thick and wavy and it never seemed to stay in place. We were not the tallest of gents, but we were built strong and stout. We could run and jump and move quicker than many had ever seen. From the eye of most folk, my dad and I were very much the same.

I guessed when they'd finally got their fill of me, they would give a nervous snort, and then a cocky grin would waft across their face. Sometimes that was all. Other times they would break out in laughter, realizing I was neither a threat nor a challenge. Slowly they'd walk away, glancing back a time or two and laughing some more. A few, occasionally, who heard the mention of my name, would run off in utter disbelief or complete fear - I never knew the difference.

But then there were a select few who would seem to feel a deep primeval urge to prove their manliness. Or maybe they would suddenly develop a hankering to settle an old score for some long lost and nearly forgotten ancestor. Those who laughed and walked away were never a bother and those who ran were a welcome relief. It was the bunch that wanted to fight that wore on me the most.

"So, you're Mike Fink!" they sneered. I could see a cloud of confidence overpower them as they turned a shoulder toward me, glaring through eyes gleaming with the vision of conquest. I watched as their chests swelled and their fists clenched tightly.

Did they think that whipping a fifteen-year-old boy would be a trophy? These were grown men or near men who had visions of saying to all within earshot, "I whupped Mike Fink!" They had heard who Mike Fink was, and they knew all about him. Only the most greenhorn of Easterners had not heard of my dad. Everyone up and down the Mississippi, Arkansas, Red, Ohio and Missouri Rivers, and every little port town in between knew about his propensity for fighting and how he would take on all comers.

My dad had long been dead. *When* he died was 1822, or so I have come to believe. I was around nine years old or there about, but I had not seen my dad in years. *How* he died had never been exactly clear to anyone. Of course, everyone had his own story. Some say he died while navigating the swollen Arkansas during a raging storm. Some say he died lost in the winter snow, frozen while trapping near the Rockies. Still others said he was shot by a trigger-happy acquaintance in a gunsmith shop in Fort Smith. Drowned? My dad was too good of a keelman to ever let any river get the best of him. Frozen? My dad never wandered too far from the rivers he loved, and I never heard him speak with much regard for traipsing in the snow. Shot? Well, there was probably more truth in that story than any other yarn I had ever heard.

And now, long after his death, there are those who still felt a need to get even for whatever reason. Maybe they conjured up tales from their past family difficulties with my dad. Or maybe they only wanted to prove their manhood by fighting the name only.

I just stood there and let them bob and weave at arm's length from me. They would jerk and dodge fictitious swings to their body and head. They would holler and make deep noises in their throats as they moved in circles around me. They did so much moving and swaying it would have tired out most men. I assumed that the pounding in their hearts kept them going. Most who would challenge me were bigger, but not all. Most never knew I had been in this situation on many occasions before; meaning I was not a stranger to defending myself. These adversaries often would need a little encouragement from their friends or others nearby who were more than glad to watch a fight than be in it. As the voices of the crowd began to drum into his ears, I knew the first swing was eminent. Once his arms began to throw punches, it was easy enough to dodge and back away. This, of course, would usually cause him great frustration. His swings and attempted punches grew wilder and less directed. Once he stopped to take a breath, I knew it was my time to act. The moment he blinked his eyes to come at me again, I threw - with all the might I could muster - one strong and well-placed punch directly to the side of his nose, right between his lower eye and upper lip, just to the inside of the cheek bone. This was usually enough to stop any more aggression toward me. The feller was now most likely laid out on his back, dazed and bleeding. I would pretend to be coming at him again and I would stand directly over him as if to swing with all my might one more time. This threat usually elicited a request to stop and I could walk away without causing much more of an incident than necessary.

I had to admit, in years past, there were a lot more fights I had lost than I cared to 'fess up to. Now that I had gotten older, I usually won my fair share.

I didn't know why folks thought just because my dad was Mike Fink and I had his name, that I was like my dad. Of course, when I was younger, I wanted to be just like him. It was probably because I knew very little about him. Then, as I got older and I learned who he really was, I came to be more cautious in my desire to emulate his strange and boisterous ways. And now it seemed I was just trying to survive and get on with my life, still caught in the long darkness of his shadow.

Everyone who ever lived on the river or who shot a gun at a bullseye on a tree or had hunted dinner in the woods or who had ever gone into a saloon, knew my dad. They all knew what a great keelman he was. In fact, they called him, "The Last of the Boatmen". Now, the whistling steam engines of the mighty riverboats were plying the trade along the rivers and real keelmen were no longer prized for their navigating skills as the speed of those paddlewheels could beat any keel load of boatmen. When it came to his rifling skills, he was the best shot who ever competed anywhere between the Ohio and the Arkansas Rivers. Before his river days, it was his marksmanship that fed his family and kept clothes on their backs. He would enter every sharp shooting contest there was, and he would win, too. Often, he would make more money by offering bets on the side. Those were his *good* aspects. On the other end, I had learned he was the orneriest cuss whoever walked the face of the earth. I am not sure there was ever a day that went by that he was not involved in a fight somewhere. And there are few stories of him losing one. It seemed to him that a man had to prove his mantle everyday and everywhere he went. It was like being a part of the River made a man fight all the time. As much as I did not want to be a part of that river life, I somehow had drifted towards it.

Sometimes I thought, the more times changed, the more they stayed the same. Years later, many years after his death, his legend had only seemed to grow. If you were to hear the stories later, you would hear that the fights got bigger, the men got meaner, the shots all got better and the river got wilder. What could you believe? It did not matter to me anymore. I was content to live my life and maybe one day no one would walk up to me and say,

"So, you're Mike Fink!"

CHAPTER 1

THE CAPTAIN

"Fink! What took you so long? Did you deliver the bill for me?" My boss, Mr. Morten bellowed.

I was panting from the long run to get back as soon as I could.

People can really drag their feet when they must pay a bill, and that's just what happened. At first, I thought the wagon owner was trying to skip out without paying for the load of whiskey barrels he was bringing up into the backwoods of Illinois. He hemmed and hawed about the price, but finally gave me the money. I'd seen him before. He was a very short man with a huge belly and these long suspenders that stretched down to the waist of his pants, covered by his stomach, and up and over his wide shoulders. I never knew his name, and he didn't seem like a person that cared whether I did nor not. Once I got the bill paid, I was in a dead run to get back to the boat. I knew if I was late, Mr. Morten would complain. And he did.

Before I could answer, he growled, "If you want to get paid, you best be unloadin' them barrels!"

Mr. Morten did not care who I was. I was sort of glad. He treated me like any other worker and that was fine with me. Of course, all he cared about was getting his paddlewheel unloaded and loaded. He could have had President John Adams himself as an employee and Mr. Morten would have had him earning his keep.

I had no great fondness for Mr. Morten. He was a fairly young man and had accumulated his wealth from an inheritance of his father, a riverboat captain. His father had died under strange circumstances a year or so earlier and now the business belonged to the young Mr. Morten. He was a tall, lanky man who never had a beard or mustache or any facial hair for that matter. He looked a lot younger than his thirty-five years of age. Most of the men who worked for him thought he was a sissy boy. A lot of them knew his father who captained the steamer before the younger Morten took over. When the son was still a boy, he would travel on the ship with the older Morten. Everyone thought the younger Morten was spoiled. His father always gave into his tantrums. Now that he is the captain, they would still laugh and make fun of him behind his back. But they did not mind working for him since he paid better than any other job around Cairo, Illinois.

"I ain't payin' you sorry sons of a pig to stand around, now, git busy or I'll fire the lot of you!" He yelled at the others who worked the dock in Cairo. At least he yelled at everybody without favor to anyone.

CHAPTER 2

THE TOWN

If my mom knew I was cavorting with the type of men who would work one day and be drunk for the next two or, "river trash", as she called them, she would blister my hide. From the time I could remember, my mom never spoke highly of any venture that was correlated to the River. Never mind that this little town would not even exist if the river didn't pass around it. I thought Cairo was a funny name for a city in the United States. Our teacher at school had told us about a very old and ancient city in Egypt also named Cairo. Were we named after that city? She talked about the desert and the pyramids and she told us about a river that made that town important. She called it 'The River Nile'.

Here at home, the story goes that crop failures up north forced the folks there to come to Southern Illinois to get food, like corn and other vegetables. It was a lot like in the Bible, when Joseph's brothers had to go to Egypt to get food. This part of Illinois became known as "Little Egypt". Did we get named Cairo because we were in Little Egypt or did our name Cairo make people call this part of the state Little Egypt? I guessed I would never know.

Cairo was not an old city. It was founded in 1818 by a man named John Comegys from Baltimore, and another man named Bond. My mom said my dad moved us here because Cairo was said to become bigger than Louisville or Cincinnati or even St. Louis. He told her we could find our fortune here. So far, it had become just another broken promise. Being on the convergence of the Ohio and the Mississippi wasn't the answer that many folk thought it would be.

It wasn't just the Mississippi and the riffraff associated with it that my mom was worried about. Although not as big, the Ohio ran into the Mississippi just below our house on the southwest end of town. My mom felt the Ohio carried its own set of dangers and dangerous sorts who worked its waters. Yet, somehow, the Ohio just never captivated my attention like the mighty Mississippi.

Located where the two rivers forked together, Cairo was a stopping place for travelers and river men and a lot of shady folks who traveled up and down the river in search of fast money. They didn't find it here. Many passed through and went on to bigger towns. Few people stayed to live here.

I continued to work the cargo for the ship. I unloaded the barrels and crates to be shipped north towards Effingham County and beyond to Champaign and the east to Indiana. Staying busy gave me plenty of time to let my mind wander about my dreams of one day leaving Cairo and finding my future. My thoughts were quickly interrupted when I heard the smack of a whip against human flesh. It was a sound that made my stomach flop every time I heard it.

CHAPTER 3

THE SLAVE

"Did you sass me, boy? Did you?" Mr. Morten's foreman was an evil man. My dad might have been mean at times, but Jack Mills was downright bad to the core. He raised his short whip up into the air over his head ready for another blow.

"No sir, I ain't sassin' you, sir, Massa Jack," answered the deckhand named Cletus. Cletus was a slave, not much older than me, but double my size. Maybe triple. However, when compared to Jack Mills, Cletus looked awful puny. Mills was the biggest man I had ever seen. Although my dad was in many fights, I couldn't say the same about Mills. He never got into fights. Because he was so big, no one ever wanted to test their luck against him. What stories were told about his encounters in fisticuffs always ended up with a man dead. With stories like that, not many wanted to fight him and wind up the same. Mills had a bushy black beard, a wide, bumpy nose and lips that protruded, almost swollen-like, out from under his mustache. You could barely see his eyes between the whiskers on his chin and the hairy, dark eyebrows that made one black row across his forehead from ear to ear.

"There's one thing I don't take to, boy, and that's sass! Do you hear me?"

Mills was about to lash Cletus' back again when Mr. Morten yelled, "Mills! He ain't no good to us bruised and bleedin'!"

Mills stopped just short of laying that whip against Cletus. When Mr. Morten turned to head back to the boat, Mills could not control himself and kicked Cletus right in the rear; hard enough to send him flying off the plank and into the river. The splash of water caused Mr. Morten to jerk around and I heard Mills say,

"He slipped!" With that, all the others who were working the dock began to laugh.

I glanced down at Cletus and I saw him struggling in the water. I realized he couldn't swim. I waited to see if someone was going to throw him a rope, but the men just kept on laughing and carrying on with their work. Cletus was not a friend. I barely knew him. But I could not let him flounder in the water and maybe drown. His splashing became more frantic and his struggle only made it more difficult for him to stay above the water. At the same instant, I heard Mills.

"You, Fink, get back to work!"

When I didn't move, he yelled again, but this time I did not hear what he was saying. I eased the barrel off my shoulder and onto the plank. Then I dove into the water. Cletus saw me and flailed wildly with his arms to reach me. I tried to grab him and pull him to shore but he kept splashing the water and I couldn't get a grip on his body. I thought if he did not stop and let me help him, he would surely drown, and drag me down with him. I was becoming tired myself of having to fight him and I knew the river undertows could pull you down in the blink of an eye. Before I could think, I landed a punch to his face that sent him into a shocked daze, and he finally relaxed his arms. I was able to grab him around his chest and pull him to shore. Once I could touch bottom, I grabbed his hands and pulled him the best I could up on the bank. He was so big and heavy, more than half of his body was still in the water, but at least his head was out and he would not drown. He couldn't catch his breath as he kept coughing spurts of river water out his mouth. With one great heave, he spewed a gush that came out his mouth and nose. He blinked several times, opened his eyes and looked at me angrily.

"You hits me!" He complained as he rubbed the jaw that I had punched moments earlier.

"I saved your life, you ungrateful, good-for-nothin' –," I was ready to tell him off when I heard Mr. Morten call to me.

CHAPTER 4

THE REQUEST

"Fink! Git up here! Right now!"

It sounded like he was mad at me. I just couldn't make anyone happy. As I dragged myself up the steep bank and to the plank that led to the boat, I could see Mr. Morten motion for me to follow him up to the boat. Once he got on deck, he paused and waited for me to join him. When I got there, he grabbed my arm and said,

"Let's go talk on the other side."

I knew he was going to yell at me for what I did and I was prepared.

"Mr. Morten, I don't know what came over me. It was just like - well, I couldn't help it, and I promise I will never –,"

"O shut up!" he interrupted. He glanced all around as if looking for anyone who might be listening. Still holding my arm, he looked me square in the eyes. "I'm grateful for what you did. None of those other galoots out there would have given a pig's eye for that boy."

He paused for a moment as if wondering what to say next.

"Look, believe it or not, I like that boy. He is one of the best workers I got. I don't care what I give him to do, he can do it. He's strong as an ox, and he catches on fast. Only trouble is, just like all slaves, he ain't got no book learnin'."

I stared at Mr. Morten, wondering what he was getting at.

Seeing my consternation, he blurted out, "I need you to teach that boy some learnin'. You're a smart boy. You got book learnin', ain't you?"

"I've been to school if that's what you mean." I didn't mention it was only for one year, and that was two years ago. It's not that I didn't like school. It was something to do and I seemed to learn fast. But, with my dad gone, I felt I needed to work and help support my family. My mother didn't complain much. If it wasn't for the times Mr. Morten would stop by and buy my mom's vegetables and some baked goods, we wouldn't have much. He never sent anyone to pick up the goods, but always came by himself. My mom seemed to trust Mr. Morten and he treated her nice. I guessed that's why she didn't mind me working for him. Often, he appeared to pay more for the food than I thought they were worth, but I never said a word.

I waited to see if Mr. Morten was going to say anything else. After I thought about it for a moment, I wondered aloud, "Why me? Why not anyone else?"

"You saw those men out there. They'd just as soon left him to drown. You think they're gonna want to help him learn?"

I reasoned not.

I paused for a moment to gather my thoughts. Mr. Morten must have figured I wasn't too keen on the idea.

"Look, if it's the money you are worried about, I'll pay you, same wage you are getting now," he said.

Actually, I wasn't even considering the money aspect. I was thinking there wasn't a whole lot I could teach another being.

Deciding it couldn't hurt to try, I agreed. "Sure, Mr. Morten, I'll give it a try. When do you want me to start?"

"Well, just hold your horses. There is just one little problem. You can't let anyone know what you are doing. Understand?"

He paused, waiting for me to agree, but I really didn't understand.

He answered for me. "Look, if word got out I was paying someone to teach a slave to read and write and do numbers, I'd lose all the business I have up and down this river. You gotta keep this quiet. Now, do you understand? If anyone finds out you're teaching that boy, you'll not be working for me ever again, and I will make sure no one will ever give you a job on this river - ever!"

Before his little speech, I wasn't sure I wanted to do the job, but now he had scared me, and I felt like I better do it or else.

"Yes sir, I understand," I replied.

Mr. Morten looked up across the river into the western sky where the sun was setting. "Well, it's after quittin' time. You come see me tonight, late; and bring that boy with you. We will talk more details then. Now, git!"

CHAPTER

FINDING OUT ABOUT CLETUS

Later that evening, I returned to the boat as it was lashed against the docks. The river looked glassy calm as the Cairo Queen sat motionless and majestic. I enjoyed watching the riverboats up and down the river. Yet, somehow, it was not a life I thought would be for me. Maybe it was my dad who spoiled it for me. How could I love the boats but hate the river life? Surely this was not going to be my future. But now, it seemed to be all I could ever hope for.

Mr. Morten's boat was not the biggest on the river. Far from it. But it was fast and easily maneuvered. I loved watching the paddlewheels as they churned the water into a frothy force, pushing the ship along the river. I could smell the black smoke billowing overhead as it settled, and it filled my nostrils with a whiff that somehow, even against my own will, drew me to the river.

As I boarded, I noticed everyone was gone except Cletus. He was still stacking barrels neatly up against the inside wall of the main deck. I could see into the pilot house above, but I did not see Mr. Morten.

"How come you never learned to swim?" I asked as I neared him. I guessed he did not realize anyone else was on the boat because he jumped when he heard my voice. He took a deep breath and glanced down toward the water.

"Ner' needs to. I ne'er fell in da water 'fore," he answered. If he hadn't fallen in, I wouldn't have been in the water either. Come to think of it, that was the first time I had been in the river in a very long time. Though I had to be on the water to work, I just didn't want to be in it.

"How long have you been working on this boat?" I asked.

"E'er since my daddy died. Prob'ly a few years now. I ain't sure."

If I was going to teach Cletus, I felt like I needed to know a few things about him. "Where did you grow up?"

"I grows up in Nawlins." He pointed south, across the bow of the boat.

"Nawlins? You mean New Orleans, don't you?"

"Dat's wat I's says, Nawlins."

"Right," I muttered under my breath. This teaching thing might be more difficult that I had hoped for. "Hey, ain't New - I mean, *Nawlins* on the river? Surely you learned to swim there."

"Oh, no, I ne'er likes da riber."

"Why not?"

"Well, I ne'er gets to see my daddy much, but af'er short visits wif da family, the boss man always comes an' git 'im and he always be drags off to da riber. Yes, sir, the riber took my daddy, I's ain't wants no part o' it."

"Is your daddy dead?"

"Yes, sir, I's tells ya, the riber took my daddy. Massa Mills says my daddy drown'd, and I's ain't wants no part o' it since."

Cletus quickly went back to lining up the barrels that had been brought on board the boat. I stood there thinking about how similar we were. We both had lost our dads and neither one of us was very fond of the river. Yet, here we were, working on the river - the very thing we hated the most.

"I have something to tell you and you must never tell another living soul about what I am about to tell you. Do you swear on your father's grave you will never tell?" I raised my right arm hoping he would agree and follow suit.

"Massa Mike, I's ain't swearin' on my daddy's grave. My momma taught me dat swearin's wrong. But she also says I's gots to keeps my word, ifn' it was man-to-man and we shakes on it. My momma says we gots to keep our promise 'fore God."

He stretched out his massive arm and I looked at his huge, callused hand before me. For the first time, a broad grin came across his face as he waited for me to shake his hand.

I was almost afraid to put my hand in his. I figured he could squeeze the life out of me if he wanted. As we shook hands I sighed in relief. His shake was firm and genuine, and I felt like he could keep his word.

I looked up, seeing a smile plastered across his face almost as wide as the river, with teeth gleaming white in the dim light. "Why are you grinnin'? I ain't told you anything yet."

"I ain't ne'er had ta shakes a hand 'fore, ya knows, man-to-man, and on a promise, and it feels real good."

A *promise*, I thought. *Does anyone keep them?*

His grin seemed to grow even wider, and we both just stood there, looking at each other.

"Well, Cletus, ain't you just the least bit interested in what I was going to tell you?"

His grin suddenly changed to a look of astonishment. The quick change of his demeanor caught me off guard and it made me nervous fast.

"W-what's wrong? W-what happened?" I asked. I did not want a fella the size of Cletus to be mad at me.

"Y-ya says my name!" he whispered, still with that astonished look on his face.

"Well, that is your name, right? I mean, everybody has a name; and Cletus is your name, ain't it?" I said, trying to recover some control of the situation.

"Yes, sir, Massa Mike, Cletus is my name, but nobody calls me Cletus."

"Nobody?" I questioned. "Not even your family?"

"No exactly," he paused, but quickly added, "but, once Massa Morten calls me Cletus. But nobody else 'til ya jes now."

"What do people call you, if they don't call you by your name?"

"Mos' time dey call me 'boy' and dat's all right, and sometimes dey call me 'blackie' and I don't mind, but," he stopped as if he was in pain and his face contorted before he continued. "When I's hears dem call me 'nigger', I know somethin' bad's 'bout ta happen."

He seemed very sad and for some reason, I felt sorry that nobody used his name.

"I tell you what," I blurted out to try to liven the conversation, "I'm calling you Cletus. That's your name and that's who you are and so—"

Before I could get out another word, Cletus grabbed me around the chest and squeezed me so hard I couldn't get another breath. I was barely able to whisper,

"L'-let g-g-go!"

As soon as he heard me, he released my body and jumped back. I collapsed against the boat cabin and took a deep breath to fill my lungs again with air. At the same time he released me, he began to apologize for what he just did.

"Oh, sir, I's so sorry! I-I-I ain't meanin' it! Please don't bees upset! I dozen't know wat makes me do dat! I am - ,"

"It's all right," I interrupted. "I'm fine. I'm not mad." I coughed then I started to laugh. Cletus was not too sure what to do. I continued to laugh and took deep breaths. After he realized I was fine and I was not going to get him in trouble, he began to laugh with me.

When I finally stopped laughing, I looked at Cletus and held out my arm as if to ward him off. "Well, Cletus," I said, putting special emphasis on his name, "I need to tell you what I was going to tell you earlier, before we got into this name thing."

"Yes, sir, I's promise ner ta tells. No one, not a livin', breathin' soul; here or no wheres round 'bouts, up riber, down riber or any -,"

"All right!" I yelled. "I believe you! Now shut up and let me finish."

"Oh, yes, sir, yes sir!" he said as he straightened up and looked at me intently.

Just as I was about to tell him, I stopped, realizing he kept calling me *yes, sir*. He even called me Massa Mike. That had to stop.

"Look, I don't think you need to keep saying 'yes, sir' to me and you definitely don't need to call me 'Massa Mike'. My name is Mike and your name is Cletus. So, from now on, just call me Mike. Understand?"

"Yes, sir, I understands!" He was broadly grinning again.

"And no yes, sir, too! Understand?"

"Right, yes, I understands." But his broad grin quickly changed to a frown and he looked concerned, shaking his head. "Ac'ually, sir, I's ain't sure I's can do dat. Der's a lot of boss men around here and if'n dey heard me call you 'Mike' or not gives you respect by sayin' 'yes, sir' and 'no, sir', why, dat could cause me a great amounts of grief." He paused, sighed and continued, "So beggin' your pardon, sir, I's must declines ya generous proposal. Ya must still bees 'Massa Mike', sir." His huge burly body sunk down as he sat on a barrel that was behind him.

For the first time, I saw the true difference between Cletus and myself. Not that he was bigger and stronger than me, or even that I was more educated and knew how to swim, but the real difference that set us apart– a difference in status; a difference not easily overcome. It was a difference I did not like. It wasn't a difference that was the fault of Cletus, or me. The more I thought about it, the angrier I became. But then it occurred to me that we were both like prisoners - he, because he was black and I, because I was a Fink.

Cletus must have seen the look on my face as he interrupted my thoughts.

"Ain't much ya cans do about dat, sir. Dat's da ways lifes is an' it always bees da way lifes is. It ain't changed for my daddy an' it was da same for his daddy. It ain't changed for me, an' if'n I's have chil'ren mysef, it ain't gonna change for dem."

I was not sure I liked what Cletus was saying. Maybe it was that way for his dad and his granddad, but if Cletus could get the learning he needed, he could change it.

I stood up and puffed out my chest. I felt renewed vigor for my plan to teach Cletus. Maybe it would mean a change for me, too. If he could learn, he could change. For me to change? I don't know what it would take. I guessed I would always be the son of Mike Fink.

"Cletus," I proclaimed, "don't be so sure it ain't gonna change."

I looked around and realized how late it had become. I knew my mom would be expecting me by now. "Meet me here in about an hour. I'm going home to eat and I'll be back. I have something to tell you then."

Cletus was puzzled, but nodded and said, "Yes, sir; I's ain't goin' nowheres. I gonna bees right here waitin' for you, yes sir. Right here, Massa Mike. Ya finds me right here, a'waitin'."

I slowly reached out to shake his hand and he took mine in both of his hands. This time he didn't squeeze as hard, and he whispered, "Tank ya, sir."

I pulled my hand away, nodded and walked down the plank. I looked down at the spot where I pulled Cletus out of the water. Somehow, I thought to myself, this day might not only change the life of Cletus, but it might change my life as well.

CHAPTER

HEADING HOME

As I walked back to my home, I started to think about my life up to this point. I had come to believe that this was as good as it could get. I was pretty much on my own. I worked along the crossroads of the two rivers, loading and unloading the boats and wagons that used Cairo as a jumping off place. Much of what was shipped out came from the farms in Southern Illinois – corn, grain, potatoes, oats, beans and apples. Mr. Morten would go south to the major ports like Memphis, Vicksburg, and New Orleans for some of his goods to ship. But he said he would go to Washington, Louisiana, which was more than thirty miles west of the Mississippi on Bayou Courtableau to pick up much of what his ship was unloading – whiskey and rum along with cotton, sugar, rice and molasses. There were a lot of cattle coming in from Texas to that town, but he never hauled them – too much trouble he would say. Mr. Morten said the Washington port was the largest between New Orleans and St. Louis.

Some boats only worked the Ohio. Some only worked the upper Mississippi and some the lower. Even the ones who plied up and down both ends of the river would stop for supplies and to take on help. I never could get on with a boat - there were too many older men to hire on with and I never got a chance. I could do the work, but not many wanted a 15-year-old on their boats. I knew some 15-year-old boys who would be regular crybabies if they were away from their mommies and daddies, even for just a day. I figured I could handle it, but I never did press the issue. I could do my work at the docks, and still be home for my family, though I knew I could be away from them, too. I just never really wanted to. Then again, I really didn't like the river. But what else was there to do?

There was a time in my life when I was not as content as I had become. I hardly ever remembered my dad being around for me. Oh, he would come home occasionally. At first, I would be glad to see him. He was a big, burly man and his size, compared to my own, always kept me in awe. He would reach behind me, grab just below the straps of my overalls, and lift me above his head. I felt like I was flying and all the world belonged to me. When I was about six and I would hear him speak, I always thought he was talking to me. But later, when I looked back over those years, I tried to remember what he said and how he said it. I had come to the conclusion that he wasn't talking *to* me at all. Looking back, I believed it was never really to me. I knew it was just gibberish, river talk, the nonsensical utterances of a drunken man.

I remember listening to the tales he told about his adventures on the river. Everything he talked about had to do with the river - riding up and down the river, racing on the river, stopping along the river - always about the river. Even when he talked about the many fights he had, it still had to do with the river. He would fight about the width of the river and its length, and about its depth and its color. He would fight about the size of his boat, how fast it went and how much it could carry. He would fight about the size of every port town and the size of the men in them. There seemed to be no river he did not know everything about; no town on its banks and no bar in those towns he did not know intimately. When you are six or seven years old, any tales from your father seemed to fill your head with wonder and an unexplainable urge to be just like him. I wanted to be, in every way, like him.

It wasn't until I got into that year of school that I started to see my dad differently. Some would say I started to see my dad as he really was.

After the last time my dad left, I never remembered my mom talking about him - ever. I never knew much about love between a man and a woman and, I guess I still don't, but as I see it now, my dad did not seem to show a lot of affection to my mom. I remembered how she would seem to tense up when my dad walked through the door, and she seemed relieved to see him go. Maybe not, but that was the way I felt it was. Somehow, through the years, I had learned that talking about my dad was not the thing to do. She would ignore the comment or just avoid answering, or even walk out of the room. I learned never to bring up his name around my mom. Of course, she was the only one who was like that. Everyone else I had ever met always gave me an ear-full about my dad. I never had to ask questions. People would just offer their stories. After a while I got tired of hearing them. Oh, at first I wanted to know more, but it seemed like every time in every story, there was always something about my dad doing something bad. I would be hurt and get mad or I would try to defend him. As I got older, it became harder to think of a good word for him. Soon, I would not even listen or acknowledge the comments I would hear.

And of course, as I got older, there were always the fights. Now, under the cover of darkness, I could move about without having someone challenging me every step of the way.

As I walked into the door of our house, I could see my mom busy over the fire. My mom was an attractive woman. Her long, straight black hair was tied back and I could see the silhouette of her face. Her skin was smooth and pale, yet her features seemed hard and cold. I knew she loved me, but I just wished she would say it sometimes. I felt she treated me like she treated my dad – cold and distant, never smiling, not looking at me when we talked. A hug now and then would have been nice; a smile, an encouraging word. I didn't believe my dad ever expected any of that, but I did. Maybe I reminded her too much of him.

My mom did not trust anyone. I was surprised when she allowed me to work for Mr. Morten, but only when he was docked in town. He would ask about her often, but he did not mention her today.

"You're home late," she said without looking up. "Your brothers are already asleep." She dipped her ladle into the pot over the fire and scooped out a pile of potatoes and gravy. She held it up and looked over to me. I then realized she was waiting for me to bring her my plate that was sitting on the table. I quickly grabbed it and held it near the ladle.

"I hope this is enough for you," she continued, as she served my plate. "I have to save the rest for tomorrow."

It never was enough. At least she had baked some biscuits and had made my favorite - egg butter. Egg butter was so easy to make even I could do it. I would take a cup of molasses and put it in a skillet with a lump of butter the size of my thumb. Then I'd beat it all together. Sometimes, Mr. Morten would give us a little nutmeg, or sometimes a cinnamon stick, and if we had it, I would add a little to the butter and molasses. I would have to stir it all together very fast when I added the egg, or it would cook in big pieces. Once the egg butter was smooth, I'd pour it over my biscuits, nice and hot. I had grown tired of going to bed hungry every night long ago. Little did she know that now someone else was helping me not to go hungry.

7

CHAPTER

MRS. BIRD

If I only ate the food my mother gave me, I think I would have starved to death long ago. I never mentioned it to my mom before, but every day I worked the docks, I would pass Mrs. Bird's house and she would have a loaf of bread for me. She would cut it open and spread cream butter and blackberry jam on it. Sometimes she used apple butter or crab apple jelly, but I liked the blackberry jam the best. Most people didn't like the seeds in their jam, but I did, and Mrs. Bird knew it. It would be wrapped in newspaper and I would tuck it into my shirt on the way to work. I loved to feel its warmth against my chest. Of course, I always had to stop for a moment to greet Mrs. Bird.

She was a very old lady, but she seemed to be very smart, and she could take care of herself. I was told she had lived in that house since she was born and her family had lived in it for many years before that. Her house was here long before the town was here. I had heard stories about how her family had made lots of money from trapping years ago. From the beginning, I thought she felt sorry for me. At first, I thought it was because when I passed her house, I would stop and tell her how good her bread smelled. I figured she thought I was hungry and I was just trying to get some of her bread. Every day she would invite me up to her porch for a piece and soon she was giving me the whole loaf with butter and jam. But after a while, I began to think it wasn't because I was so hungry or that I told her how good her bread was. I soon believed it was because I was Mike Fink's son.

One particular day she seemed to want to talk to me more than usual.

"You turned out to be a mighty fine young man, Michael," she had said to me. No one ever called me 'Michael' except my mom, and that was when she was mad at me. Mrs. Bird never got mad at me.

She had looked at me with a half grin, half frown on her face. "When I first saw you as little boy, I thought to myself, 'Oh, dear, that child will never have a chance,' but I do believe you are turning out just fine. Yes, just fine."

It had been the first time she had said anything about knowing me since I was young.

She had paused for a moment. I could tell there was a lot more she wanted to say. I could see her lips moving but she wasn't making the words. I felt like I needed to thank her.

"Thank you, Mrs. Bird," I said, but quickly added, "I mean, for the bread. You always make the best."

I had started to walk off, but her words stopped me dead cold.

"I used to make bread for your father." Her voice sounded almost like a cry.

I slowly turned around and faced her. I was sure the look of wonderment on my face did not go unnoticed.

"I prayed for your father many, many times. When he was younger, he passed here too, just like you do." She started to chuckle. "Even now, you startle me sometimes."

"I startle you?" I asked.

"Oh, yes, you do. You look so much like your father, sometimes I think it is him, coming again for a loaf of bread."

"You gave my father bread, too?" I was very interested in what she had to say. For once, I felt like someone could tell me something about my dad that didn't have anything to do about the river or fighting.

"I mean, you knew my dad?" I was intrigued.

"Oh, yes, I knew *his* parents. We were friends. Your grandfather worked for my father. My father bought many a pelt from your grandfather and your father. I knew your father as he was growing up." She was now sitting in a rocker and slowly began to rock, and a wide smile came across her face.

"He was a rascal, your father. Oh, I never saw such energy in a young boy. Sometimes I would see him for several days in a row, and then I wouldn't see him for months and months. He was always hunting all through these woods. He would travel miles and miles from home just to hunt. Back in those days, we had a lot more game - squirrels, rabbits, deer, turkey. He would always bring me something - usually a squirrel or a rabbit. Once he skinned it, and even before he would sell the pelt, he would clean it and get it ready for the pot!" She laughed aloud. "He would come back later, after I had time to cook it and he would sit out here and eat it all! What a growing boy!" She leaned close to me. "He could have cooked it himself, but I think he liked the bread I would always bake with it." She laughed some more then took a deep breath. The smile was soon gone from her face as she continued, "That was a long time ago. Times change, and people change, too." She had this distant gaze on her face, and I thought it was time for me to leave. As I took a step back to ease away from the porch, she started again. "But you, Michael, you doing well?"

"Yes, ma'am, I am. I still work at the docks." As I had turned around to face Mrs. Bird, our eyes became locked in a deep stare. After a brief moment, I felt like I needed to continue. "The money really helps my family."

"Yes, I am sure it does. And how is your mother, Victoria? Is she doing fine?"

I was even more surprised that Mrs. Bird knew my mother's name. I told her that my mother was doing fine. But as I watched Mrs. Bird, I felt a sadness in how she asked about my mom.

"I never see your mother anymore. Does she get out much?" she asked.

"No," I answered, suddenly feeling uncomfortable, like I was going to hear something I didn't want to hear. "She works the garden and takes care of me and my brothers. She has her chickens and she sells the eggs and some of the vegetables to a man who comes by every other week or so. And Mr. Morten always stops by. He buys a lot from her, too."

Mrs. Bird nodded, and then she stared intently at me for what seemed a long time. "May I pray for you, Michael? I feel God has great plans for you. I want you to remember that. Is it okay if I pray?"

I was caught off guard, for a moment, but I agreed. Mrs. Bird reached out for my hand and I moved forward to give it to her. She then grasped my hand in both of hers and began to pray.

"Dear Lord, I continue to lift Michael up to You. I pray Your watch care over him. Protect him from all harm and danger. Guard over his ways and his every step. Keep him safe for your service. Bless him and his family. Keep them close to You. In the precious name of Jesus. Amen."

Before she could say anything else, I told her I had to get to work. I thanked her for the bread again, and for the prayer, waved good-bye, and off I ran.

I didn't know why I was feeling so uncomfortable when Mrs. Bird began to talk about my mom. As much as I was uncomfortable talking about her, I wanted that much more to hear about my dad. For the first time, I didn't hear horrible things about my dad, and I was very curious to hear more. And the prayer – it somehow gave me a feeling of great peace in my heart, like God was really watching over me. I never knew much about God. My dad never went to church. I remembered going when I was very young with my mother, but something happened that made my mom cry and she never went back. Of course, since she didn't go anymore, I didn't either.

CHAPTER

SUPPER THAT NIGHT

At the table, I had already finished most of my dinner, including the biscuits and egg butter. I was still a little hungry and wished I had something else to eat. Suddenly, I remembered I needed to be back to the boat to find Cletus and to talk to Mr. Morten. I jumped up and started out the door.

"Whoa, young man, where are you going?" My mom asked. She and I had not said much to each other since I got home and *now* she wanted to talk.

"Mr. Morten asked me to meet him tonight. He had something important to tell me."

"Important?" she asked with a quizzical look on her face. "And just what might that be? What is so important that you must run out of here without hardly saying a word to me?"

I stood with my hand on the door handle, ready to leave, but she wanted a reason. Mr. Morten had asked me not to mention the reason to anyone. I wondered to myself, *Did that include mothers?* I hesitated for a moment to see if I could come up with a reason she might believe. I needed a reason that was not a lie and I could keep my promise to Mr. Morten. But I must have hesitated too long because my mom said:

"No, I don't believe Mr. Morten has any reason to see you this late at night. So, just march yourself off to bed. It is already very late." She just stood there, waiting for me to let go of the door knob, turn around and head to bed.

I couldn't believe she was refusing to let me go.

"But Mom, I promised Mr. Morten. He is depending on me."

"Then tell me, what is so important?"

She waited for an answer. *What was I going to do? Should I tell her or not? Would she even believe me if I told her the truth?*

"Mr. Morten needs me." I was struggling to find a reason without telling her the truth. All of a sudden I blurted out, "He said he has a gift for me, and he didn't want the other men to see him giving it to me. That's it. He wants to tell me about a gift he wants to give me. And he didn't want me to tell anyone. But I guess it is all right to tell you, Mom. Yes, that's it." I stopped and watched her face to see if she was going to believe me.

"A gift? You expect me to believe Mr. Morten is going to give you a gift?"

"He promised me Mom, he did! Why would he lie to me about a thing like that?"

As I continued to watch, I could see I was winning my argument, but I still needed to drive the point home.

"I won't be long, I promise. You'll see. You will hardly know I was gone at all." I continued to watch as she took a deep breath. She was giving in!

"A gift? Hm-m-m. You know all I have to do is ask him the next time he comes around?"

"It's the truth, Mom, it is! Can I go?"

She nodded in the affirmative and I could hear her as I ran out the door, "You hurry straight home, do you hear me?" The final words faded in my ears. I doubt she could hear me as I replied.

"Yes, ma'am!"

CHAPTER 9

THINGS ONLY GOT WORSE

I didn't really tell a lie. I mean, Mr. Morten *did* want to see me, and he *did* ask me not to tell anyone. But, the gift? I am not sure how I will get out of that one.

For some reason, the night seemed even darker than normal. As I walked briskly through town, there was an eerie feeling of quiet. The streets were empty and I could only hear muted, distant sounds that I could not distinguish as man or beast or other. It seemed to make me walk even faster to the dock on the other side of town. As I got closer, I could see dim lights on the boat ahead but I did not see Cletus anywhere. I thought he would be watching and waiting for me. I stopped right at the beginning of the walk and glanced around looking for Cletus in all directions. *Where is he? He promised he would meet me here!*

I began to walk slowly up the plank. For some reason, the quiet of the night made me feel I should not be making much noise myself. As I stepped onto the boat, I could hear voices. I was relieved, thinking that Cletus was already here. Just as I started approaching the top of the steps to turn toward the pilot house, I was suddenly grabbed from behind. It felt at first as if a huge tree had wrapped its thick branches tightly around me. I couldn't move. My arms were pinned to my sides and my mouth, nose and eyes were covered by what I now realized to be a massive hand. I struggled to move but I could not loosen my arms. I tried to yell, but I could not even hear my own muffled attempts to speak. I tried to turn and see who had me forcefully bound, but the sheer power that had me in its grasp held my body immoveable.

Next to my ear, I could feel hot air in slow, almost controlled, breaths across my neck.

"Sh-h-h-h," I heard a voice say in an almost inaudible tone.

My eyes were darting back and forth to try to get a glimpse of my attacker behind me, but I could not. I continued to struggle against a force stronger than I had ever felt before.

"Sh-h-h-h," I heard the voice again say in that same still tone.

This time, I forced myself to relax, and as I did, I felt the grip on me relax, too. The hand slid down my face, but was still across my mouth. Now I could turn my head, and as I slowly twisted my body around, I could see the face. It was Cletus. I tried to talk, but his hand was still pressed so tightly that I still could not speak.

Again, I heard, "Sh-h-h-h-h", and this time I kept my mouth shut.

I looked at Cletus; my face twisted with confusion. He grabbed my arm and pulled me down. He pointed to his ear and then pointed to the pilot house. I still heard the voices, but this time, I tried hard to understand what was being said, and who was saying it.

Slowly, Cletus released his grip and I could breathe again.

We both squatted and pressed our ears against the wall of the pilot house. One voice I recognized immediately. It was Mr. Morten. He was talking loudly, as usual. The other voice I could not make out. I shrugged my shoulders and Cletus made a big ugly face and cupped his hands around his chin, as if he had a big beard. Suddenly I realized it was Mr. Mills! They were arguing, and it sounded loud and angry.

"I told you she was gonna be mine!" Mills bellowed. I could imagine his face contorted and his teeth locked tightly together.

"I don't believe that is what she told me." Morten sounded like he was afraid. I had never seen him back down to anyone. Of course, when he sat in his cabin most of the time and had someone like Mills to do all his dirty work, he didn't have much opportunity to be confrontational with anyone - not that he wanted any. It now seemed like he and Mills weren't seeing exactly eye-to-eye.

"She will believe what I tell'er to believe!"

Mills' booming voice began to scare me. I figured Morten was too busy to see me tonight. As I started to ease away from the wall, Cletus grabbed me again. He looked me square in the eye and nodded for me to stay. With his grip on my arm I was not going anywhere, so I shifted my weight and leaned back against the wall and continued to listen.

"Mills, I think we should settle this like gentlemen and let the woman choose."

Woman? I mouthed the word to Cletus, and we both shrugged our shoulders. Mr. Morten and Mr. Mills were fighting over a woman! Who would have believed it. I thought to myself, *Who could she be?*

"You need to calm down. I can tell that you are not willing to listen to reason. We should continue our discussion in the morning."

Morten seemed to be trying to be rather diplomatic, although weakly, but it seemed Mills did not want any part of it.

Mills then began to laugh. It was that same evil laugh he had when he was about to do someone in. It was the same laugh he had when he kicked Cletus into the river.

"You and your daddy are just the same. Two spineless little weasels. I never liked either one of you. No, Mr. Morten, we are not waitin' till mornin'. We are goin' settle this now, tonight."

Mills laughed again, but then we heard him scream, "You and your father! Two peas in a pod!" We heard him spit against the wall where we were listening. "He wanted to wait until morning too, the worthless piece of –"

"What are you saying, Mills?" Morten interrupted, and now his voice became angry.

We heard Mills grunt. "Yeah, it was true; your father *did* have a little accident - with a little help!"

There was a long pause. I guessed Morten must have been stunned as he realized exactly what Mills confessed. "You!" he screamed. "It was you! You killed my father!"

"Don't be so high and mighty. You got his boat, and the business and all his money. I figured you might be a bit easier to deal with than him."

"I'm going to the sheriff!" Morten screeched.

"You're not goin' anywhere!" Mills yelled and then we heard what must have been Morten hitting the ground, crashing through tables and chairs.

"You got your boat and your money, but you ain't gettin' the woman." There was a pause that seemed like forever, then Mills added, "But this time, *I'm goin'* get it all! I'm gettin' the woman *and* your boat!"

"What do you mean? You would have to kill me first!"

There was total silence for a brief moment and then we heard the cocking of a pistol.

"No! No! Don't shoot! I'll give you what -,"

"BAM!"

The gun went off and everything became awful still. Suddenly, we heard the clopping of Mill's heavy boots. I didn't know what overcame me, but I jumped up and bolted for the shore. I tried running as fast as I could but my foot slipped out from under me. I landed flat on my face, on the cold, damp deck. As fast as I fell, I tried to jump up and run, but I felt a hand grasp me around the throat, and lift me up and off my feet. At first, I supposed it was Cletus. *Why is he grabbing me?* I thought to myself. I couldn't breathe and I tried to grab the fingers from around my throat. Air couldn't enter my lungs and I began to gag. I was being lifted by my neck, and my legs were dragged across the floor. I struggled to pry the fingers from around my throat. I was desperate for a breath of air. Once back into the pilot house, I was thrown down on the floor. I continued gasping for air, sucking it in to fill my lungs. Pushing myself off the floor, I rolled to the side, and there next to me was the dead body of Mr. Morten!

It was Mills who had grabbed me. He started to laugh, "Well, well, you just made this very easy for me, Fink! I couldn't have planned this any better. Who would have ever guessed you would be here tonight!"

I rolled over and sat up, facing Mills. My eyes slowly rose to see his eyes glaring into mine. "Wh-wh-what do you mean?" I choked out, trembling.

"You just got me off the hook for killin' Morten," he smiled big and I could see his rotten teeth.

"What are you talking about?"

"My alibi. Why, you came here tonight, under the cover of darkness, and you and Morten got into an argument. You saw his gun on the table and you took it and you shot him."

"That's a lie! You killed him! No one will believe you!"

"No? Why, I just might become a hero. I heard the shot. I came runnin' to see if somethin' might have happened to my wonderful boss, and I find you, standin' over the body. We struggle, the gun goes off and you are dead, too. I can hear them talkin' now.

'Ya heard about Mills? Tried to save his boss from that good-for-nothin' Fink boy!'"

Mills started to really laugh now as I was looking up the barrel of his weapon.

"Any last words, Fink?"

"Yes. You are not going to get away with this!"

Now he was mad. He bent over and shoved his face close to mine.

"No?" he snarled, "Thanks to you, I will come out of this smellin' like a rose!"

As he laughed again, he stood back up and lowered the gun, pointed directly at my heart. "Good bye, Fink. Killin' you will be just as good as killin' your daddy. Until your daddy came along, I was king of this river and all the others. But your daddy wanted to fight and I'll never forget how he beat me and took my feather. Now, I am takin' his son's life!"

CHAPTER 10

WHO COULD SAVE ME NOW?

I shut my eyes tightly, waiting for the explosion from the gun. I jerked as I heard a loud crashing sound, thinking the trigger had been pulled. But when I opened my eyes I saw it was Cletus, busting through the door. He lunged and threw his arms around the neck of Mills, knocking the gun from his hand. Cletus had a tight grip, but Mills struggled free. Mills pushed him backwards and Cletus fell to the floor, flat on his back. Mills quickly rushed towards Cletus. As he prepared to pounce on him, Cletus lifted his feet and pressed them against the charging body of Mills, catching him right in the stomach. The advancing force of Mills continued and Cletus pushed his feet up, forcing Mills to go flying past his own body, through the door and over the railing - landing on the ship's boiler deck below. There was a loud crash and then silence.

I jumped up and ran over to Cletus. He was still lying on the floor of the cabin. He was breathing hard and fast. I tried to speak, but the words were stuck in my throat. Cletus reached up for me to take his hand and help him up. I pulled with all the strength I had left, but I could not budge him. He waved me off, rolled over, pulled himself to his knees and then to the standing position. Both of us were still breathless.

Finally, I could speak, "Is he dead?"

"It don't matter. I's gots to get out of here!" gasped Cletus. He had to hold on to the side of the cabin for support as he stumbled to the plank.

"Wait, you can't leave!"

"Why not?"

"We just witnessed a murder!"

"And who kilt who?"

"Mills killed Morten! We heard it!"

"And who kilt Mills?"

I paused. I knew what Cletus was thinking. "It was self-defense! You saved my life!"

"An' whose gonna believes you, a 15 year old boy, a Fink no less?"

I thought to myself, *Yeah, who would believe a Fink?*

"But you saw what happened," I pleaded with Cletus, "You are a witness!"

"Well, ya knows wat? Slaves can ne'er be a witness! Ya knows dat! And even if'n we could be a witness, dey will believes you 'fore dey believes me." Cletus sighed loudly. "If Mills founds lyin' der dead, who ya tank dey'll hang fer it?"

Cletus turned and headed for the shore.

"You can't go alone."

Cletus stopped and turned around. "Ya goin' wif me?"

"We are in this together."

"Do wat ya wants. I's gettin' outta here!"

I turned and looked down at Mills. His body was lifeless. Morten was dead. Mills was dead. I turned back to see Cletus running to the north of town. He was almost out of sight. I took a deep breath and began to run after him. I thought to myself, *Yep, we are in this together.*

11

CHAPTER

FUGITIVES ON THE RUN

It was hard trying to catch up with Cletus. As big a man as he was, he could really run fast. I figured if my life was on the line like he thought his was, I would be running just as fast, too.

When I did finally catch up with him, he wasn't ready to slow down. I pleaded with him to stop and rest, but he would not listen.

"Cletus," I said in between panted breaths, "Let's - stop - and - rest - please!"

He did not heed my request. I finally could not run anymore. I came to a large cottonwood tree and fell against it. My body was too tired to even stand and I slowly slumped to the ground. *Cletus would have to go on without me*, I said to myself. My body was sprawled on the ground and my head rested on a root. My eyes were closed but I quickly opened them when I heard the snapping of twigs nearby.

They found us, I thought. How did they do it so fast? I thought we could run north and then east all night, and just before light, cross the Ohio into Kentucky before anyone would discover the bodies. I was too tired to even try to hide. I wasn't going to help them find me, but I wasn't able to get away either. The cracking of twigs was very close. Whoever was trying to find us, was not very quiet themselves. I laid there in the damp night waiting. It sounded like they were right on top of me now. I looked up and who did I see, but Cletus stomping around the tree in the pitch darkness. He didn't see me! He must have come back to find me. As he passed me in the dark, I leaned up and called out his name.

"Cletus."

You would have thought he was shot out from a cannon the way he jumped and yelled! He spun around and fell near my feet.

"Ya almos' scares da black off me!" Cletus pulled out his kerchief from his back pocket.

"What were you doing?" I asked.

"I's lookin' for ya! I's thought ya bees lost!"

"Me? Lost? This is my back yard. I know these woods like I know the palm of my hand! Admit it, you were the one that was lost!"

"Well, I's ain't wantin' to leave ya. Ya *did* say we's in dis toget'er."

"Then why didn't you stop when I begged you to?"

"I's wantin' ta git as far away from dat town as fas' I could!"

"But why did you come back?"

Cletus flopped down next to me and leaned back against the trunk. He turned to me and said sheepishly, "I ain't knowin' where I's goin'."

"So, you *were* lost!"

"No, I's ain't *lost*! I 's knows I's in da woods. I's jest ain't knowin' where ta go next."

We sat in silence for a moment. We could hear the distant croaking of frogs at a nearby pond. They and the chirping crickets were the only sounds in the night. The brief rest was good. I was ready to continue. Cletus jumped up first and reached down for me. He jerked me up and I was standing in a heartbeat.

"So, Massa Mike, where to now?"

"Hey, you can stop with the 'Mister or Master Mike' stuff. Whatever you're saying. Ain't no one around to make any difference."

"Whatever ya says, sir!"

I glared at him for a moment and then he added,

"Ya leads da way, Massa Mike!"

The stop gave me a moment to realize I was all scratched up from all the brush we ran through. I thought Cletus would be torn up as well. I couldn't tell in the darkness and he wasn't complaining. Maybe his mind was more on getting away than on anything else. Without thinking, I had jumped into the lead. I wasn't going as fast as Cletus did and I could feel him right on my heels.

"Dats as fas' as ya can goes?" he asked.

"I can go faster, but I'm trying to find a deer run through here. Once we find that, we will follow it east, to the river and we will make a lot better time."

"What's a deer run?" asked Cletus

"Well, deer are creatures of habit. They find a place of food and they go back every night until it's all gone. They create these paths through the woods and sometimes a herd of five to over ten will run these trails and beat the ground smooth. They break off weaker branches and dead limbs with their antlers and so it feels like you're running through a tunnel."

Cletus did not seem so interested in my explanation about the deer run. He seemed more concerned about getting caught.

"Won't we bees headin' close back ta town?" I could hear the concern in Cletus' voice.

"Believe me, the deer don't want to get any closer to town than we do."

Just at that moment I hit the clearing. "I found the trail, Cletus. Stay with me. We'll be at the river before dawn."

Cletus didn't say a word, but as I picked up the pace, he stayed right with me. The ground was hard and smooth, just like I figured. We ran as fast as we could without any brush or branches to block our way. I hadn't realized how bright the night had been. The moon was not nearly full, but the sky was clear and the stars were as bright as I had ever seen them. It seemed to give enough light for us to see our way and make for an easy run down the trail. Everything was going smooth, but then . . .

I heard the blast of a muzzleloader and felt the flying bark hit my back. I figured it was shot off the side of the tree I just passed. I knew that a second shot would not happen right away, since the shooter would have to reload with powder and a ball before he could shoot at us again.

I hit the ground and wondered if Cletus was all right. I slowly crawled around to face behind me, and I whispered out his name softly,

"Cletus!"

He didn't reply.

"Cletus, are you hit?" Still nothing.

I started to ease back to where I thought Cletus might have been. I had slithered along the ground for about ten feet when I felt a hand reach out and grab my arm. It was Cletus. He was hiding behind a tree.

"Why didn't you answer me?" I whispered, "Are you shot? I thought you were shot!"

"Dey gots me! Dey gots me!" Cletus was straining to whisper.

Cletus let go of my arm as he sank back behind the tree. In the shadows, it was darker, but we could see the path clearly. It would be difficult for anyone to see us, and we would see them first. We laid there motionless. We could hear voices and they were coming closer.

"I's ain't gonna let dem catch me. I's gonna git hung fer sure!" Cletus pulled away from me, but as I tried to hold onto his arm, his strength just pulled me along with him.

"Wait! If you run, they will catch you for sure! Just wait!"

Cletus relaxed and settled back down on the ground.

"I's trustin' ya, Massa Mike Fink," his voice faded out as we both took cover, lying flat to the ground in a thicket near to the path.

At first, we could not make out the voices, but as we continued to listen, they became more distinct and we could understand what they were saying. It sounded like two men and they were almost standing over us.

"I told you, you missed him!" said the first one. His voice was high-pitched and he sounded whiney.

"Didn't miss him either! I saw him real good!" This one's voice was deep and sounded like he had gravel in his throat.

"Then where's his body, if'n you shot'im?"

"I know he's here somewhere."

They were both poking the barrels of their guns around the trees and into the underbrush on either side of the deer run.

Now one was almost standing right on top of us. He was reloading his gun when he bent over and looked at the base of the tree right by us.

"Look, it's blood! I told you I got him!" It was the deep-voiced one.

I watched as he rubbed his hand across the tree.

"Here, looky at this," he said and walked over to the other one and shoved his hand into whiney one's face.

"Smell it, Marvin, ain't that blood?"

Marvin pulled his head away and curled up his nose.

"Well," he said, "it looks like blood Thorton, but your hand smells like you been crawlin' around the floor of the chicken coop!"

"He's here, Marvin, I can sense it! Keep lookin' and keep quiet!"

"Me keep quiet? Yer the big mouth!"

"Sh-h-h-h!"

Just at that moment, everything got deathly quiet. I just knew they were going to find us and drag up back to town; if they didn't try to hang us right there in the woods.

The two men were frozen in their tracks. The silence seemed to go on forever. All I could hear was the swelling of my chest as I breathed in and out. I couldn't even hear Cletus. I slowly turned my head to face him and I couldn't believe my eyes. Cletus was either sleeping or he was out cold! I didn't want to try to wake him or he would make noises and we would be found.

The two men were still standing motionless. I watched as they slowly turned their heads side-to-side trying to listen for the slightest sound.

Then, without warning, out from the brush about ten feet from us jumped the biggest buck I had ever seen! His huge hooves hit the ground right in front of Thorton, startling him and making him fall backwards. Thorton spread his arms to try and balance himself, and his fist hit Marvin right in the face. They both crashed on the ground across from us.

Thorton screamed out, "That's him! That's him! I knew he was here! Get up, Marvin!

He's wounded, and I wanta git'm!"

I watched as both of them scrambled up and ran off in the direction from where we just came.

After they were out of earshot, I rolled over and started to laugh. *Deer!* I thought to myself. *They were after deer! Not us!*

"Cletus, wake up! They're gone! They were after deer, not us!"

Cletus didn't move. I reached to grab his arm to shake him, and I felt something warm and wet.

Blood! Cletus was bleeding!

He *was* shot! Did he pass out or was he dead?

CHAPTER 12

CLETUS WAS SHOT

I tried to see where Cletus was shot, but there was not enough light coming through the brush. Since I knew the two hunters were gone, I crawled out from under the bushes and pulled Cletus with me into the moonlight so I could see his injury. I grabbed both of his hands, dug my heels into the ground and pulled with all my might. He didn't budge. I knew I had to help stop the bleeding or he would bleed to death from the wound - if he wasn't dead all ready.

I remembered the kerchief Cletus tucked in his back pocket that he used to wipe his brow. I reached down into the back pocket of his overalls and pulled it out. I thought I would just wrap it around his upper arm to stop the bleeding.

Just lifting his arm to get the kerchief around it was a chore. I grabbed the two ends, pulled them together, but they barely touched. So much for that idea - I couldn't get the two ends to tie. I wasn't real fond of seeing blood myself. Looking at the wound made me feel a little weak kneed, but I knew I had to control his bleeding. I started to move my hand over his arm to see where the bullet hole entered his body and try to cover it so he wouldn't bleed anymore. I couldn't exactly find it.

I pressed both of my hands against the bloody area of Cletus' arm. I was hoping I was covering the place where the bullet entered his body. For the first time, everything stopped. We weren't running or hiding. No one seemed to be chasing us. Within just a few moments, I started to feel tired. I folded my hands over Cletus' arm and leaned forward, pressing my body weight against him to put more pressure on the wound. As I laid there, my eyes grew heavier and heavier. I fell asleep within minutes.

"Where are we? Where are we? They didn't find us, did they?" I heard Cletus' voice at the same time I felt him jump up and toss me off his arm like a leaf off a dog's back. There was now a little light filtering into the woods as the dawn broke around us.

"Thank goodness you're alive!" I yelled, still sprawled on the forest floor.

"Of course, I'm alive! You thought I was dead?" Cletus sat up and leaned against a tree. I didn't recognize his voice at first. In my bleariness of a deep sleep, for a moment I thought I was hearing someone else.

"Yes! You were shot - and bleeding! I thought you would bleed to death!"

"I's 'member now! I's shot!"

Now, I recognized the voice.

Cletus turned his head and stared at his left arm.

"Not that arm! The other one!" I yelled.

Cletus slowly moved his head to glance down at his right arm.

"I's shot! I's shot! Where's my 'kerchief?" he yelled. He started to reach into his back pocket.

I handed the bloodied rag to Cletus as I moved over to see the wound. He placed the rag over the area of his arm that was now mostly just dried blood.

As I watched him, I realized there was no bullet hole.

"Wait!" I said. "Let me see that." I reached up to move the rag away.

"Hey! I's bleeding! I's might die!"

I pushed Cletus' hand away and looked closely at the wound.

"This is just a scratch! There's no bullet!"

"Wat ya means? Ya says I's bleedin' to deaf!"

"Well, you could have, if that hunter was a little worser aim."

"Hunter? What hunter?"

"Last night, remember? We thought they were after us, but they were just after deer. His shot must have missed the deer and grazed you!" A silly grin came over my face. "Wait a minute! You don't remember that, do you? You passed out!"

"I's don'st 'member." Cletus squirmed against the tree.

"Well, you did pass out! A lot of help you would have been!" I paused and pulled his hand away from the wound and looked at it closely. I glanced up to see Cletus looking the other way. Seemed like Cletus wasn't so fond of blood either!

At that moment, I remembered Mrs. Bird's prayer that God would take care of me. It could have been me, laying there, bleeding or even dying. I looked up heavenward and breathed a "thank you" to God.

 For the first time, I realized I had never thanked Cletus for saving my life on the boat last night. Here he was, afraid of his own blood, but he wasn't afraid to risk his life for mine. He had killed a man to protect me. He hardly knew me and yet he had fought the biggest man I had ever seen just to keep him from killing me.

Cletus rolled his head towards me and he caught me staring at him.

"Wat? Wat's ya lookin' at?" he wondered.

"You know, I never got the chance to thank you for what you did back there."

"Tank me? Fer wat? I ain't done nuttin'."

"No, you just saved my life, that's all."

"I's don't knows wat ya talkin' 'bout. I's ain't saves yer life."

"You did, too! Mills would have killed me, and my dead body would have been found right there next to Morten's."

"Oh, ya means back on da boat." He paused as if it was just a commonplace occurrence. "Well, I's knows nuttin' 'bout savin' yer life. What I's knows, is dat Mills a very bad man, and he kilt da best friend I's ever had."

I was dumbfounded.

"Let me get this straight." I was beginning to feel a little confused about exactly what happened. "You attacked Mills and probably killed him because of Morten, not me!"

"Well," he said, trying to figure out what I was getting at. "Well, Massa Morten bees good to me. I's ain't lettin' Mills get away wif dat. I's gots to do sumtin' - and fas'."

"Fast!?" I screamed out, "If you had been only a second slower, I would have wound up dead just like Morten! Fast? If you were so fast, then why did you wait until he had already cocked his gun and had it aimed right at my head?!"

"I's knows nuttin' 'bout dat. All I's knows I's thinkin' 'bout my plan and I's waitin' fer da 'xact moment ta ketch'm off guard and den I's attacked."

"And here I was feeling all grateful for what you did for me and all the time you weren't doing anything for me!"

"I's sorry if'in dat's da way ya feel. I's just bein' instinctual. Massa Morten bees real good ta me, an' knowin' dat Mills had kilt him. . ." His voice trailed off. He turned away from me and closed his eyes.

Well, I said to myself, *I really can't blame him.* He had saved my life, whether he realized it or not. As far as I was concerned, he did the right thing.

"You did the right thing," I repeated, but aloud. I patted his shoulder, but he did not look at me nor did he answer.

Well, God, I thought, at least I can thank you for Cletus saving my life.

I looked up and could see the sun's rays coming up in the eastern horizon, hitting the treetops in the early morning. I crawled out to the deer run and stood up. I stretched and rubbed my stomach. I felt hungry, but a quick look around made me realize there was not much food to be found. I walked a few feet up and down the run, trying to think about what we could eat. I noticed Cletus had soon followed me and he was the first to speak.

"Am ya as hung'y as I's?"

"I was just thinking about that. I'm sure we can find a bite. Let's keep walking ahead. We'll come across something directly."

For some reason, neither of us was in a hurry like we were the last evening. We walked at a brisk pace. Cletus was close behind me and neither he nor I was in a talking mood.

A glance at the sun rising in the sky, which seemed almost an hour, we still hadn't said a word, but our pace had picked up some. Maybe it was the growling in our bellies that made us run a little faster.

"Stop!" I heard Cletus whisper.

I stopped and turned to him.

"Ya hears dat?" he said.

I strained to listen, but the wind blowing through the trees masked all other sounds.

"I don't hear nothin'," I said, and I continued on the trail.

Less than ten steps ahead, I did hear something. I stopped dead still and strained to listen again.

CHAPTER 13

FINDING FOOD WASN'T EASY

It was a turkey! No, it sounded like a whole rafter of turkeys, making their gobbling noises ahead and to the left of us. I turned and motioned to Cletus, pointing to my ear and nodding. I eased up ahead and moved closer to the brush that lined the deer run. It was turkeys all right. The males were huge, or at least they seemed huge. They had bright red waddles hanging from the top of their beak. Their tail feathers were spread wide and they were prancing around like they owned the woods. I never got this close to a flock like this before. With a gun, I could be fifty yards or more away and still get a clean shot. Now, they seemed close enough to grab. I turned and waved for Cletus to come to me. I had hunted turkeys before. This should be easy. I leaned over to Cletus and whispered.

"Let's grab one. It'll be good eating tonight. You go left and I'll go right."

He nodded and we slowly crept in opposite directions. When we were about twelve feet apart, we nodded to each other again, and, at the same time, stormed into the area where the turkeys were standing.

There they were, all grouped together. *This is going to be easy,* I said to myself. I dove for the one closest to me. I grabbed only air as he scurried out of range. I landed on the ground, scaring the other turkeys. I looked up and saw Cletus chasing them through the woods. I had never seen turkeys run like that. Before, after I shot one, the others would scatter, but trying to catch them by hand was different.

In a flash, I was up and chasing the turkeys with Cletus. They were so fast! But not only fast; they were scooting around the trees, in and out. They did not run in a straight line, but they were moving zigzag through the forest. They'd run in one direction, and in a blink of an eye, they would change directions and be going in the opposite direction. I had never seen anything like that in my life. Before we knew it, they were out of sight, and both of us stopped and looked around in circles, wondering how they got away so quickly. We chuckled to ourselves later when we remembered how funny it looked to watch those turkeys running in mass around and around and in and out of those trees, and to imagine us running after them the same way. How they never ran into each other or into a tree was a surprise to us.

So much for a turkey dinner. We never thought about it before, but if we had caught one, how would we cook it? Neither of us had any way to start a fire. We were hungry and we needed to eat soon.

In the quiet as we continued to walk, I thought about my mom and home. She was probably worried to death. I didn't come home last night. The news of the two dead men would travel fast in our town. When the people in town realized Cletus and I were gone and that Mr. Morten and Miles were killed, they would be putting two and two together and figure we had a hand in it. The more I thought about it, the worse I felt for my mom. *She must be sick with worry,* I thought to myself. Without much more thought, I blurted out to Cletus,

"I got to go back."

Cletus had been walking behind me and as soon as I spoke, I heard him stop dead in his tracks.

"Ya's gonna leave me?" he said in disbelief.

I stopped and turned to him. His mouth was open and his eyes were sad. His whole body seemed to droop.

"Cletus, what we did was wrong, but running away just made it worse." I paused, but he did not respond. Cletus was still frozen in that pose.

"Look at us," I continued, "We're tired, we're hungry, we've jumped at every sound. What kind of life is that? We didn't do anything wrong. It was self-defense, and whether you believe it or not, you saved my life and that is what I'm going to tell the sheriff, and the deputies and the judge and anyone else who'll hear me."

Cletus still didn't move.

I sighed and continued to try to convince him to go back with me. "Miles had it coming. He was an evil man. He's hurt lots of people in the past. And he's killed some along the way. You're not like that."

Cletus finally changed his expression. He looked away and squeezed his lips tightly together. He breathed deeply and turned back towards me. As his eyes met mine, it felt like he was burning a hole right through me.

"I's knows we innocent, Massa Mike, but all dose men sees Boss Miles boot me into da riber. Dey'll believe I's wants revenge. Dey'll tank I's waits to ambush 'im to git even for wat he did ta me. Dey don' t care who I's saves. Dey'll only sees a black man an' a dead white man, and I's as good as dead mysef. I's might as well jest walks into dat riber and ne'er stop an' drowns mysef, 'fore I's lets 'em beat me, string me up an' let me die."

Cletus was now looking past me. I turned around to see what he was looking at and then I saw it - the Ohio! I didn't realize we were so close. I had been so lost in my thoughts about going home, I didn't recognize where we were. I quickly turned back to Cletus.

"It's the river, Cletus!"

"I's knows it's da riber, Massa Mike. I've been starin' at it!"

"This is great news!"

"Wat ya means? Great news? I's here talkin' 'bout gettin' kilt an' ya tink dat's great news?"

"No, Cletus, I mean, no, you getting killed is not great news, but the river is. There is a cabin not far upriver from here."

I started to run up to the shore and veer to the left, heading up stream. I glanced back and Cletus still had not moved from his spot. "Hurry!" I yelled to him. "I know a place where we can get something to eat!"

That was all I needed to say. Cletus broke into a run and was soon up with me. We ran along the bank of the Ohio, in and out of the trees.

My mind wandered back to those turkeys. A smile broke out on my face, and I imagined that right this minute, we must have looked a lot like those turkeys, flitting through the woods.

CHAPTER 14

AN UNPLEASANT ENCOUNTER

The cabin was one of my favorite places to go. With all the activity of the morning, I had almost forgotten about it. Of course, I called it a cabin, but it was more like a tent on stilts. It was barely enough room for one large man, let alone two. I knew my dad used it before, and many others used it too, but for many different reasons. I had used it to fish from when the water would rise high enough to flood the pits around it. Others used it to store their game while hunting before they headed out. It was often used as a place to sleep or stay out of the rain or cold. Sometimes I would find an old knife or piece of flint or an old ragged blanket left by a hunter or fisherman. There was always a line and pole pushed into the corner and hooks could be found with their sharp points pressed into the door frame. If ever I found matches to start a fire, I would always leave a few for the next traveler who may have been without. At times, I would come and there would be just one or two still left in the box, and then other times, I would find that someone had filled the box with new matches.

As we continued to run along the river, I was hoping we would find some of those matches again.

I beaded my eyes on the trail ahead, but I was startled to a dead stop by a voice behind us.

"Well, howdy, young Mike, and what might you be doin' out in these parts?"

It was a voice I had heard before but could not place. My heart sank. Turning ourselves in was one thing, but being caught on the run made us look very bad. Cletus had froze in his tracks too, and neither one of us moved as the voice continued.

"Ain't like you to be out here without your gun." After a brief pause that seemed like an eternity, he added, "And who's your big friend here? You two wouldn't be running away now, would you?"

His speech was slurred and slow. It sounded like he had been drinking a lot.

I could hear him chuckle under his breath. I sighed deeply and after composing myself, I slowly turned around. It was Old Man Coppersmith. He probably heard us coming and was hiding until we passed by. He was a trapper-hunter-fisherman-trader-boatsman-jack-of-all-trades drifter whom I had run across many times in these woods. He never came to town much, but would do anything to make a buck. Right now, I figured he was planning to turn us into the sheriff to get the reward for capturing us.

I saw that Cletus was still facing me, his eyes as big as saucers and sweat pouring down his face.

"Mr. Coppersmith," I squeezed out his name through the forced smile on my lips. He was a dirty old man who probably never bathed unless he accidentally fell into the river. His beard was long and almost all white except for two dark strands on either side of his mouth. I watched as Coppersmith raised the barrel of his rifle and pointed it straight at us. He was not the friendliest of people and I did not want to rile him nor make him trigger-happy.

I tried to start a conversation.

"Are you staying at the cabin?" I said, still smiling weakly.

To my surprise, that seemed to rile him up more as he rose from the stump he was sitting on and raised the stock of his gun to his shoulder. His eyes got very squinty and the corner of his mouth curled up on one side.

"You know I'm in that cabin! That's why you two are here, ain't it?" His voice had started soft, but it then became a loud gruff at the end.

I tried not to show any change in emotion as I realized that Coppersmith had not heard about the killings back in Cairo. He thought we were here for—*Why did he think we were here?* I thought to myself. With the barrel of a long rifle staring me in the face, I did not want to make him any angrier than he already was.

"No!" I answered quickly. "We didn't know you were here!" I glanced at Cletus, who still had not moved. "Right, Cletus?"

Cletus made very short, jerky movements with his head, nodding in agreement.

"Don't you boys lie to me! You came to steal my game, didn't you?" Coppersmith said as he moved closer to us. The tip of the barrel was right between us. I could smell his breath and the foul stench of chew and liquor blasted my face. The smell gagged me and I had to step back to get my breath.

"Mr. Coppersmith, I promise, we did not know you were here. We were hungry and cold and we thought maybe we could, uh, find a fishing pole and hooks and, uh, do some fishing for breakfast, uh, right, Cletus?"

For the first time, Cletus spoke, "Yes sir, dat's right, Massa Mike is tellin' da truf. We's hungry an' we's lookin' to do some fishin'." Cletus had not taken his eyes off me since we ran into Coppersmith.

When Coppersmith heard Cletus speak, he turned his attention to him; taking the barrel of his gun and pressing it against Cletus' jaw.

"And what are you doing out here, boy?" Coppersmith's eyes cut back to me and then to Cletus again. "You runnin' away, boy? Is that what this is all about?" He turned to me.

"You helping this boy run away, Fink? Is that right? Sneakin' a slave through the woods to freedom?"

As he said the word "freedom", he lifted the gun in the air with his arms, swinging them wildly as if proclaiming some great truth, and as he tried to step forward, he began to stumble. I watched as he fell. I saw his eyes roll back into his head and he collapsed, passed out.

Cletus still did not move at the sound of Coppersmith's body hitting the ground. He glanced down and slowly turned his head until he could see him laid out. It seemed Cletus finally took a breath.

"Massa Mike, wat's he bees talkin' 'bout?"

"Cletus, he doesn't know about what happened in town. He thought we were here to either steal his game he had been hunting or that I was trying to help you escape."

As Cletus watched the limp body of Coppersmith, he asked, "Why he bees tankin' dat?"

I knew the answer. When Cletus finally looked back at me, I decided to confess the truth.

I stumbled over the words, but I got them out: "Because, I, uh, I had, uh, done it before."

"Wat ya means, 'done it 'fore'?"

"A year or so back, I was here and I stumbled on a large stash of game in the cabin." Cletus looked at me in disbelief, waiting for me to finish my confession. "I didn't know who it belonged to, OK?" I said, trying to justify my crime. "I decided to take it back home and share it with my family. Coppersmith found out and he hasn't been very fond of me ever since."

"Ya steals dat man's meat?"

"I was young, Cletus," I answered.

"Ya wasn' dat young," Cletus glared. "But, stealin' bees wrong, Massa Mike. It says so in da Bible."

"I made a mistake. I'm sorry. I never did it again."

"Ya gots to ask for forgiveness, jes' as soon as he wakes up. And ya gots to ask God to forgives ya too!" He paused and leaned in to stare me straight in the eye. "Ya believes in God, don't ya?"

"OK! OK! I will tell him. Satisfied?"

Cletus still stared at me, as if it wasn't enough.

"Ya gots to ask for God ta forgives ya, too."

"All right." I sighed deeply and continued, looking up heavenward "Dear God, please forgive me for stealing Coppersmith's meat. Amen."

Cletus looked at me with a disapproving eye. "Ya means dat? Ya says it from ya heart? It don't sounds like it was from ya heart."

This time I bowed my head. "Dear God in Heaven, will you please forgive me? I am sorry I stole Mr. Coppersmith's meat. I will never steal from anyone again. Thank You for forgiving me," and then I added. "and help us, Lord. Help the people know that we didn't kill those men. Amen."

After the prayer, I felt better and it made me feel content everything would turn out all right. How that was going to happen, I didn't know, but the prayer seemed to help. Then, I thought about what Cletus did back on the boat. "What about you, Cletus? Don't you need to ask God for forgiveness?"

Cletus squeezed his lips together, paused a moment and then looked me in the eye.

"Ya's right, Master Mike. I's goin' pray right now." I watched as he bowed his head and tightly closed his eyes. He pressed his hands together, his fingers locked together. He began to pray.

"Dear God,

You have blessed me so much. Thank you. Lord, I did not mean to kill anyone. I know killin' is against Your Commandments and I ask Your forgiveness. Please forgive me of my sin. In Jesus Name, I pray. Amen."

There was that voice again. Cletus sounded so different when he prayed.

That seemed to make Cletus content as well as he smiled and spoke. "So, wat we's goin' do now?"

"We can't leave him here. Help me take him to the cabin. I'm sure he's just drunk. He can sober up there."

Before I could reach him, Cletus had picked him up, tossed him over his shoulder and grabbed his rifle. Cletus seemed uncomfortable carrying a rifle, so he handed it to me.

I turned to head to the cabin and Cletus followed.

The cabin was less than one hundred yards away. As we got closer, I got the strangest feeling there were others lurking nearby.

15

CHAPTER

THE CABIN WAS NOT EMPTY

The closer we got to the cabin, the more uneasy I felt. I slowed our pace and took very soft steps, watching not to step on twigs or branches. Cletus watched me as I was being very cautious and he followed suit.

"Wat's happenin' Massa Mike?" He whispered, "Mo' troubles ahead?"

"I don't know Cletus," I whispered back, "I got this strange feeling that something is not right."

"Wha' we's gonna do?"

"Let's get to the cabin, then we can figure it out."

I picked up the pace a little, thinking I was just getting spooked, but something kept telling me to be very careful.

We had been traveling the main path to the cabin, but I decided to take a roundabout way instead. I turned back into the woods and Cletus followed without question as he was still effortlessly carrying Coppersmith on his shoulder.

We continued moving in a circle around the area surrounding the cabin. I did not want to get too close until I knew it was safe to approach.

We were now almost directly on the opposite side of the cabin and back to the bank of the river. I stopped to assess the next move and I heard Coppersmith starting to stir. I laid the gun down and helped Cletus pull him off his shoulder and lay him on the ground. We were both watching the old man as he moaned, opening his eyes and quickly squeezing them shut against the bright light of the sun that was now almost overhead. He rubbed his eyes and blinked them open only to see Cletus and me standing over him. He seemed so startled that I was afraid he would yell out. I fell to my knees and pressed one hand over his mouth, and with the other hand I pressed my index finger to my lips.

"We are on the northeast side of the cabin." I whispered. "I have this feeling that something is amiss. I want to go check it out."

Coppersmith calmed down and agreed with a nod of his head. As I turned to head toward the cabin, he grabbed my arm, and reached for his gun, placing it in my hands.

"Someone's been stealing my game. I thought it was you," he whispered.

Now I was sure about my feeling. Someone *was* in the cabin.

It wasn't long before I heard voices. It sounded like it was more than one person, and if they were thieves, they were not very quiet about it. They probably would not have heard me even if I had been clanking pots through the woods.

At first, I couldn't make out what was being said, but as I eased closer and listened carefully, I could hear distinct words,

"I want the skin this time."

"No, you had the skin the last time."

"But it was too small. I want a bigger'un."

"Look, just keep skinnin'. That old geezer'll be back soon and we need to high tail it out of here."

"Start packing the meat in the boat!"

"Hey! Why do I have to always pack the boat?"

They continued to argue and I kept creeping very close. Then without even seeing them, I heard their voices and realized they were just young boys. They couldn't have been more than twelve years old; maybe younger. I quickly thought of an idea and I headed back to the others.

They were both watching for me. This time I was not very quiet heading back.

"What did you see?" whispered Coppersmith. "Anyone in the cabin, stealin' my meat and furs?"

"Yes, they're in there right now," I responded.

Coppersmith jumped up and reached for his gun I was still carrying.

"I'll blast them to kingdom come, the varmints!" As he stretched out to get his gun from me, I pulled it away. He looked up at me and glared. "I said I'm goin' blast them, those good for nothin' critters! Now, gimme my gun! Now!"

"Just a minute, we ain't going to blast anyone, least of all a couple of kids."

"Kids?" he questioned, "Kids been stealing from me? Then I'm goin' whup their hides 'til they can't sit down for a month of Sundays."

"Just a minute!" I said, trying to calm Coppersmith down. "We don't need to whup anyone. Just listen to my plan. How 'bout we scare the daylights out of them? Scare them 'til they'll never come back?"

Coppersmith sat back down and he cocked his ear to listen. "What you got in mind?"

"Cletus can you sound like a bear?"

"Huh?"

"Can you sound like a bear? You know, growl real loud and low?"

"I can try."

"Good. Now, Coppersmith, stay here and when you hear me yell out, I want you to say, 'The bear is right behind that cabin' Then shoot in the air and yell, 'I missed him! I hope no one is in that cabin!' Can you do it?"

Coppersmith smiled, "With pleasure!"

"OK, Cletus, you sneak behind the cabin. I'll head to the other side and when you see me wave, start to growl for all you're worth. Now, Coppersmith, you wait for me to yell first."

Cletus crept behind the cabin as I quickly got in place on the other side. I raised my hand to signal Cletus and he began to let out the loudest, most awful, bear-like roar I had ever heard. Then I yelled as loud as I could,

"We got the bear trapped, boys. He's headed for that cabin!"

Just then I heard a gunshot and then Coppersmith yelled. Cletus was still roaring and before we could blink, the two boys bolted out of that cabin. Their boat was just pulled on the shore of the Ohio, and in a moment, they were in their boat, paddling away to beat the wind.

Without saying a word, all three of us met at the cabin, out of breath from laughing at the sight we just witnessed.

A big smile was on Coppersmith's face.

"I thank you boys for the help. I guess those was the two that was stealin' me blind. Is there anything I can do for you?"

Cletus started to laugh aloud again.

"Why are you laughing now?" I asked.

"I was just thinkin'. If dat were a real bear, I's wrestled him to deaf, cook't 'im an' ate da whole tang!"

Coppersmith laughed, "What you boys are tellin' me is that you're real hungry. Right?"

We both nodded in agreement.

"Well then, you're in the right place."

We sat on a downed Cyprus log as we watched Coppersmith fix the meal as fast as he could. It still seemed like forever. Once he sliced off that first piece of venison, we knew the wait was worth it. And when we finished, there were not much left of that deer hindquarter.

For a moment, we seemed to have forgotten about our troubles back in Cairo. Mr. Coppersmith didn't know anything about what happened and he was not a threat to turn us in. After eating, we sat around the fire and listened to Mr. Coppersmith tell stories tell about when he grew up in the western part of Virginia. There was a lot I did not know about him and I found him to be a very interesting person. He lost his father in a mining accident when he was only eight years old, and two years later, he lost his mother to the fever. He then went to live with relatives, who moved around and each move brought them further and further west through Ohio, Indiana and then to Illinois when he was only eleven. Within a few years, most of his family had passed and he'd been on his own ever since. Each stop in his life yielded great stories with many adventures of hunting, trapping, fishing and life as he lived it. Some were so funny we laughed and laughed. Other stories were so sad, I thought we might tear up. He never married and never had his own children. He said he's still not sure if he wanted to stay in Illinois or move on.

"I hear there's great hunting in western Missouri. I gest might try it," he said.

Before we knew it, hours and hours had passed by. The sun began to set, and its golden rays danced in the ripples of the Ohio. Once our bellies were full, and we finally stopped to breathe, we realized how tired we really were. A lot had happened in the last twenty-four hours. We didn't speak about it but I knew we both felt like tomorrow would be another adventure.

CHAPTER

THE OHIO

The strong smell of venison brought me instantly awake. As I sat up, I could not see much in the dim light of the pre-dawn. I heard voices and I could see the brightness of the fire lighting up the trees around me. I felt the thick smoke as it blew into my eyes.

"Mornin' Massa Mike," I heard Cletus bellow. I rubbed the sleep and the smoke from my eyes and I could see him and Coppersmith through the flickering flames of the fire, sitting side by side across from me.

"Massa Coppersmith still laughin' 'bout what ya did yes'erday."

"It was a good thing you two came along," Coppersmith seemed serious to me. "Had it been up to me, why, I was so angry, I'd shot first and talked later. Humph! I'd had the law after me for killing those two wet-behind-the-ears scallywags." Coppersmith got up and poured another cup of coffee from the pot sitting on a rock near the fire. "How was I to know they's only boys? Wouldn't matter, I guess, killing somebody is killing somebody."

Cletus and I look at each other. Coppersmith was hitting too close to home. Such talk was making us uneasy.

"So," he continued slowly, "It ain't much of my business, but what are you two gonna do now?"

He stood there and looked back and forth at both of us, waiting for an answer.

Cletus seemed not to know what to say, so I blurted out, "We're headin' down river. Memphis, maybe New Orleans. We're looking for work."

Coppersmith smiled broadly and said, "You and a –" He paused just a moment to look at Cletus, "a slave? Like I said, it ain't none of my business, but you two ain't out here lookin' for a ride down the river. You coulda done that in Cairo." He paused as if trying to figure out what we were really doing in this neck of the woods.

"Naw, you two boys' in trouble. I mean, look at you. You're out here with nairy a bit of food, nothin' packed for a trip, in the middle of nowhere and you, Fink - out here without your gun? Yep, you're in trouble. Am I right?"

Cletus and I did not know what to say or do. Should we confess and tell the truth or lie? Before we could speak, Coppersmith started again.

"Well, I ain't askin' for an answer. You boys helped me an' I owe you. You want to go down the river? Then all I can do is help you."

Coppersmith stood up and looked up the Ohio.

"There's a keel up the river, about an hour from here, maybe more. I ran into him yesterday before I met up with you boys. Rather tense and uneasy sort of fella. He had barrels of liquor and I traded some game meat for a jug. Seems like his keelmen got drunk, and ran it aground. Asked me to head down river with him. He needed some boatmen, since his crew got too drunk to work and he fired them."

"I told him I couldn't help, but . . ." He looked at us both. "You two want the job or not?"

We both stood up and neither was sure of what to do.

"Well, git goin'! I got you up early so's you have time to catch him before he leaves."

I started to take off, but Cletus paused and looked at me. "Ya gots sumtin' to says to Massa Coppersmith?"

At first, I didn't understand, but when Cletus glanced back at Coppersmith, I realized what he meant.

I walked over to Mr. Coppersmith and said, "I want to ask your forgiveness for stealin' your meat a while back. It was foolish of me and I'm sorry for doing it. Can you forgive me?"

Coppersmith had this mean look on his face that seemed to last a long time. I was not sure what he was going to do or say. Finally, he burst into a grin. "You turned out to be a mighty fine young man, Mike Fink, and yes, I will forgive you. And thank you for what you did for me yesterday. Now…," Coppersmith lowered his eyes and pointed up the river.

Cletus and I looked at each other, but before I could say anything, Cletus quickly turned north and began to run up river. I wasn't sure if staying on the run was the best idea. The keel would be heading right back toward Cairo. Would we turn ourselves in then, once we got to town? Would we try to sneak past and continue our escape? Whatever the decision was going to be, I decided, right now, to follow Cletus.

Before I could turn to run, Coppersmith tossed me a slab of cooked venison. "Thank you, Mr. Coppersmith, I guess we're going to try to catch that keel."

Running toward the bank to catch up with Cletus, I heard Coppersmith yell out to me, "Remember to tell'm I sent you!"

CHAPTER 17

FINDING A WAY DOWN RIVER

I could not see Cletus, but I had lost him before in the woods. I wasn't worried until almost an hour into my run, I heard a gunshot ring out and flinched. At first, I did not know where it was coming from. Was Coppersmith hunting? The water always carried sound so good. Maybe it was someone shooting from across the river. The morning was calm and the water on the river was slick like glass. I increased my speed as I ran along the river, trying to listen for another shot, to see where it was coming from. I didn't even hear birds chirping or the wind rustling the treetops. *Is there going to be another shot?* I kept running, but then the second gunshot went off much closer and made me duck in fear. I moved behind a tree that leaned out over the river. From the shade of the tree, I got its location. It was definitely up ahead. Then it struck me that it was coming from the direction Cletus had been running. Gunshot or not, I needed to find Cletus. Although the trail was clear, the shoreline had thick brush growing out of the water's edge and on the other side of the trail, it was thick as well. If I was the target, I seemed well protected. I continued to run until I heard a voice ahead.

"You're not to steal any of this cargo from me, you hear me? I know you're out there, you untrustworthy, thieving mischief-makers! So, you best be on your way. I am an excellent marksman and if you force my hand, I shall shoot you!"

I was expecting to hear another shot fired so I dove behind a tree. As I raised my eyes to see what was happening, I saw Cletus standing over me.

"Get down! You'll get shot!" I yelled.

"I's ain't gonna gets hit! He couldn't hits da broad side of a barn if'n he's a-leanin' up agains' it!" Cletus grinned widely. "He musta hears me runnin' up to 'im t'rew da woods and he's been shootin' ever since."

About that time, I heard another shot, but Cletus didn't even act like he noticed.

"Are you crazy! You're a pretty big target! And I'd say you're about the size of a barn, too! Now get down!"

Cletus ignored me, and turned back toward the shots. I slowly crawled up next to Cletus and looked in the direction he was staring. Through the thick bushes and trees, I saw a man standing on the deck of his keel, trying to reload his gun. I glanced at Cletus and back at the boatman. I watched as he took forever to load the powder in his gun. If we had been after his cargo, we could have just walked up to him and pulled the gun out of his hand, before he could get off another shot.

"I'm warning you! I know you're out there! I'm deadly with this type of armament! You better be gone before I get this reloaded! I shall not be responsible for any injury I might inflict upon you!"

I couldn't believe how inept this man was with a gun. I watched as he continued to try to pour the powder from his horn. He was so nervous, he was spilling it all over the deck, and missing the barrel completely. I could see lead shot scattered everywhere. Then I saw two other rifles. That is why he could fire off three rounds so quickly. Now he had to reload and he was having a hard time doing it.

Cletus looked at me, shook his head and chuckled. "Massa Mike, he ain't even comes close to hittin' me!"

After witnessing the man fumbling as he tried to reload, I knew we were not in much danger. I motioned to Cletus to follow me and we both headed to the boat in plain sight.

"So, there you are! You don't believe me, do you? Just you wait!" he yelled as he continued trying to reload. I knew he did not have a shot in the barrel, so I was not in fear of us getting injured. He would look down to the barrel he was trying to fill with powder, and quickly look up at us as we approached him. At the same time, he was backing up. Right behind him was one of his other guns, leaning against some crates.

"Look out!" I hollered, but it was too late. As he stepped back, his right foot caught on the stock of one of the guns behind him, and his left foot caught the barrel. Before we knew it, he had tripped backwards, dropped his gun in the boat and then plopped into the river. Cletus and I ran to the boat and we both looked over the side, but we couldn't see him. He had already disappeared beneath the surface. Just at that moment, we saw his head bob up about five yards downstream. I looked at Cletus and he shrugged his shoulders.

"I's can't swims," he said.

Of course, I knew that, I remembered. With that, I leaped into the water, and in a moment, I had the man by his shirt collar. When I turned around to paddle back to the boat, Cletus had found a rope and was tossing it to me. I grabbed hold to it and he pulled us both to the bank.

As I crawled on shore, Cletus grabbed the gentleman and dragged him up to dry land. He was choking, coughing, gasping, and spitting up so much water, it seemed like he must have drunk half the river.

We just stood there watching him. He was a very skinny man, with a long pointy nose. His hair had been so slicked down that the fall into the river didn't even mess it up. His clothes were soaked, as were mine, but there was something strange about his garments. They reminded me of what a preacher would wear for a Sunday morning meeting. When he finally got his breath, he looked dejected and gasped,

"Okay, you win, just don't hurt me. Just take what you want, but leave me alone. I won't try to stop you."

Cletus and I looked at each other. We had no idea what he was talking about.

"Sir," I said, "I don't know who you think we are, but we are not here to steal your cargo. We're looking for a job. We heard you needed some help, so here we are."

Cletus and I smiled at each other and when we looked back at the man, he had the most surprised look on his face.

"You're not thieves? You're not here to steal my cargo?"

"No, sir. Mr. Coppersmith told us about your dilemma and we just happened to be available to help you move your keel downstream."

"Mr. Coppersmith?" he asked. "Oh, you mean that ornery-looking fellow from yesterday? The smelly one? The one with that awful meat and disgusting smell of tobacco on his breath?"

"Yeah, that Mr. Coppersmith. He told us how you lost your keelmen. How you fired them for being drunk on the job."

"Is that so? I mean, is that what he said?"

"Yep, so here we are to help."

When I turned around, Cletus was busy picking up kindling for a fire. When I started to ask him about how we were going to light it, he had reached into his pockets and pulled out a handful of matches.

"I's ain't gonna jump in da water wif dees," he smiled. Cletus must have seen the box back at the cabin and put some of them in his pocket.

As the gentleman started to stand up, I reached my hand down to help him. When he saw my hand, it startled him at first, but he grabbed it and pulled himself up.

"Do you young fellows have names?" It was the first calm tone he used with us.

"Yes. My name is Mike and this is my, uh, this is Cletus." I didn't know if I should have said *friend* or *slave* or whatever, but I did not want to raise any suspicions, and by all appearances, it did not.

"My name is Calvin Blackwater of Philadelphia, and I am pleased to make your acquaintance; and," he added, glancing back at the river, "I am extremely grateful for your daring rescue. I would have met my Maker a lot sooner than I had ever contemplated. Bless you, young Mike."

Before I could speak, I smelled the smoke from the fire Cletus had started. Mr. Blackwater and I moved to the fire to dry our clothes. I took off my boots, shirt and pants, and was down to my long johns. Then I went looking for branches I could use to stretch my clothes over so I could prop them up near the fire. I was too busy to notice that Blackwater had not removed any of his wet clothes, except for his shoes.

"Dem's clothes ain't gonna dry too fast still on yo' back," Cletus fussed, pointing at Blackwater.

"Oh, yes, of course," he said. He seemed embarrassed. He slowly turned away from us and began to unbutton his shirt, cutting quick glances to see if we were watching. I was not sure I had ever seen a man so timid about undressing in front of other men. With his shirt off, he held it in front of his chest as he eased to the edge of a nearby tree. As soon as he reached it, he jumped behind it and began to remove his pants. Had he just stood there in the first place and disrobed, we probably would not have noticed a thing. But when he turned shy, it caused us to be more inquisitive. When we heard him trip and fall, trying to get his leg out the pants, we both had to turn away to avoid laughing aloud.

Cletus and I continued to pick up kindling and to make small talk about the woods and the river, when we realized that Blackwater was still behind the tree.

"Gentlemen," we finally heard Blackwater say, "I'm afraid I must ask you to step away for a moment. I-I-I must step out and place my garments near the fire. Would you be so kind?"

Cletus and I turned our backs to the tree and stepped on the other side of the fire; far enough that we could not feel any warmth from it. We sat down, shaking our heads, and chuckling to ourselves.

"Thank you. I-I'm not in the habit of disrobing in public. This is quite contrary to my normal practice, and it makes me somewhat uncomfortable. I do hope you understand."

"Ye'sir, Massa Blackwater, we'd ne'er wan'ta makes ya uncomf'a'ble," said Cletus, surprising me with his humor and still smirking about the situation.

After several minutes of silence, brought on by our hesitancy to say anything that would start us laughing again, I asked him a question.

"Begging your pardon sir, but I have the feeling you've never keeled before. Am I right sir?"

"You are quite right young Mike. Whatever gave you that impression; the way I was dressed?"

"No."

"The way I handled a gun?"

"No."

"Then the fact I could not swim?"

Still facing away from Blackwater and the fire, I said, "No, it was none of those, sir."

"Ah, yes, you Westerners think you are the only ones who can keel a boat. I know, you think of us Easterners as not having the grit to be keelmen. Am I right?"

"Well, sir," I tried to be diplomatic, "I've looked around and I don't see your poles. There just ain't a way I know of to navigate this boat without them; unless there is some newfangled way you Easterners discovered, that us 'Westerners' hadn't learned about yet."

We sat waiting for a long time before Blackwater finally answered.

"They, uh, got stuck in the mud just upstream. I didn't have the strength to pull them out. I lost both of them that way. I drifted for over an hour or two yesterday, before I ran aground here."

"I am sorry to question you sir, but some of your story and the story Coppersmith told us just don't seem to add up."

"You are right, young Mike. I have not been fair with you two. You risked your lives to save me. You could have done me much harm, but you didn't. I owe you my life and I owe you the truth."

I turned around without thinking, and to my surprise, he was fully dressed. His clothes were still not completely dry.

"Come, sit near the fire and I will tell you the whole truth."

CHAPTER 18

THE WHOLE TRUTH

"My name is Calvin Blackwater - well almost. What I meant to say is, my title is Reverend Calvin Blackwater. I am, or was, the Associate Pastor of the Mount of Olives Baptist Church in Philadelphia, Pennsylvania. That's the truth. My church collected funds to send me west to found a new congregation. I was to build a church in a part of the country where I felt we needed to spread the Word of God."

"Dat sounds mightily fine, Reverend," Cletus said.

"Oh, but it is not 'mightily fine', my dear Cletus," moaned Blackwater.

"Then why don't you take your funds and head back home, and try another time," I interjected.

"Oh, if it were that simple, my young man. You see my 'funds' are sitting on that deck before you."

"In dem crates an' barrels? Doze looks like whisky barrels. Massa Coppersmith said he traded game fer ya whiskey. Was dat a lie, too?" asked Cletus.

"It is a long story," Blackwater looked dejected.

"Well, we have plenty of kindling, our clothes ain't dry yet and we can't go anywhere without the poles."

"An' we ain't gots food, too," Cletus reminded me.

"Oh, yes we do." I grabbed my pants off the branches near the fire, reached into the front pocket and pulled out the large hunk of smoked venison Coppersmith had given me.

I pulled off a long strand of it, handed it to Cletus and then I pulled off a piece for myself, tossing the rest to Blackwater. It had the taste of river water but Cletus and I began to chew on it anyway. Blackwater was still holding it in his hands, smelling it and curling up his lip as if I had given him poison.

Cletus told him, "Ya gots to eat up, Massa Blackwater. We ain't got nufin' lef'."

With that encouragement, Blackwater started taking small and then larger bites, until he was eating it as fast as we were.

It wasn't long before we had finished the venison and Mr. Blackwater began his story again.

"Those are whiskey barrels; you're right, Cletus, and I am quite ashamed to tell you that. I am even more ashamed to tell you that I was hoodwinked into buying them. I was told they were supplies to be delivered to Memphis and I could sell them for three times the money I would spend on buying them in Pittsborough. I never considered anyone would lie to me, cheat me and then try to steal from me. They told me they were dry goods, cloth, preserved foods – items desperately needed further west and I could make triple my money.

"I thought, with all the money I would be making, I could build three churches. I never questioned anyone. The two that sold me the barrels said they would help me down the river, since I had no idea how to sail." Blackwater looked at the keelboat and added, "Well, not sailing, there are no sails. I mean," he paused, "I know nothing about boats!"

"We were not out of Pittsborough barely a day before I found out what I really bought! I was furious! The two just laughed at me. Little did I know they had planned to pick up a friend to help them travel downriver and then they would have killed me or left me somewhere for dead!"

"Well, how did you get away?" I asked.

"God took care of me," he answered.

"How did that happen?" I quizzed.

"You see, the men liked the whiskey they had on the boat. The night before last night they were sitting on shore and got so drunk, they passed out. I was able to push the boat out into the river and escape. I'm sure they never thought I would attempt such a blatant exodus. I did not get far after losing my paddles, or sticks, or whatever they are called."

"Let me get this straight. You were shooting at us because you thought we was them and they had tracked you down and were trying to get your boat and your cargo. Is that right?"

"Sorry. I was mortified. I'm glad neither of you were injured during my shooting spree. They may still be out there, looking for me right now. But how will we escape?"

"Don't worry. First light tomorrow, Cletus and I will be looking for your poles. If they're stuck in soft mud, they can't be too far off shore. They should be easy to get."

"I's ties a rope to ya an' holds da udder end on da shore, Massa Mike," Cletus remarked quickly.

"Great idea, Cletus." I looked around. "It's getting dark soon. I doubt we'll have any trouble tonight. Let's get some sleep and get an early start in the morning."

Without any further discussion, we all laid down near the fire and fell asleep. Little thought had been given this day to the events that had happened back in Cairo, in what now seemed ages ago. Little thought tonight was given about what would happen tomorrow, either.

CHAPTER 19

THEY CAME
AFTER BLACKWATER

I awoke to another morning with the wonderful smell of food cooking over a fire. This time it was fish. Cletus had two catfish with a branch run through them, hanging over the fire. He had the skins peeled off and the smell was wonderful

"Where did—" Before I could finish the sentence, Cletus told me proudly.

"I's may bees big, but my hands's fas' as lightnin'."

"You caught those with your hands?"

Our conversation woke Blackwater.

"What is that horrible smell?" he asked.

"Fresh catfish, Massa Blackwater. It don't gets much better'n dis," answered Cletus, as he pulled the fish off the saplings and let them fall on a nearby rock to cool.

Blackwater watched with a wretched look on his face as Cletus split the biggest fish between us, and we began to peel the steaming white meat off the bones.

"Dis'un's fer ya, Massa Blackwater," Cletus said as he pointed to the other fish, "It's whole lots tas'ier when it's pipin' hot."

"Thanks, but no. That meat we had last night is still sitting in the pit of my stomach." Blackwater groaned, and stood up. "Are you sure you will be able to get the poles? If they come after me, and I imagine they are the type of men who don't give up so easily, I'm a dead man, and so might the two of you be."

"Well," I said, looking at Cletus, "I think we can take care of ourselves."

"Just in case, you better take this," Blackwater said, as he handed me a rifle with the horn and shot. "It's not loaded," he then added, "I think I should stay." He turned and handed the other gun to Cletus. "You might need this one."

The look on Cletus' face told me he was still uncomfortable holding a gun in his hands. He seemed almost afraid to take it, but he reached out and grabbed it. He was holding it as if it was a fine china teacup. I watched him as he stroked the smooth, oily finish on the barrel and as he ran his hands across the hardwood stock. He was holding it far out in front of him, like a baby with a wet diaper.

"It ain't gonna bite you, Cletus," I teased, grinning up at him.

He didn't look at me; but he soon brought it close to his body, clinching it tighter, admiring its power.

I need to teach that boy to shoot, I said to myself.

I decided to load all three before I would leave. "By the way, how did you wind up with three?" I asked.

"Both of the men had one and they brought one for their partner," Blackwater answered.

"You took their rifles? Good for you; but for them, I guess they're hopping mad by now."

After I loaded all three, Cletus and I began our search for the poles. We had not walked one hundred yards when we found both of them - lodged in the roots of the trees growing out in the shallows. The current must have pulled them out of the mud and they floated downstream and into the roots. These were probably the same roots that caused the current to send Blackwater's boat into the ground in the first place.

Just as we safely had the poles on dry land, we were both startled by the sound of voices - angry voices, not too far upstream; and they were closing in fast.

"It must be the two Blackwater spoke about," I whispered to Cletus. "Let's get back to the keel."

Silently, we raced back to the place where we had camped.

When Blackwater saw us, he knew something was the matter. "Are they coming?" he asked.

"Yes. I believe it's them. Cletus, pull the boat back upstream about twenty yards and make sure it is safe on shore. Blackwater, put out that fire and cover our tracks the best you can."

"What is your plan?" questioned Blackwater.

I had to come up with an idea of what to do quickly. "I want them to think you fell off and drowned."

"Da boat's moved, Massa Mike."

"Good, Cletus."

"I tried to make the scene as natural as I could," said Blackwater.

"Grab your guns and let's hide behind that clump of trees - and be quiet!"

I was hoping they would not notice our camp downstream. We were not far from the boat and Cletus had made sure it would not float away. I was also hoping we would not have to kill them to save ourselves.

The wait wasn't long. They soon found the boat.

"Looky here Jethro, jest like I tell you! That tenderfoot done got stuck."

The first one was dressed in clothes that seemed much fancier than he ought to have had, but they were covered in dirt. He was tall and lanky and had long hair that almost covered his face. It made him look wild and dangerous.

"Where is he, Amos?" The second one was short and had to take big steps to keep up with the tall one. He was just as dirty as the first, but his clothes were much shabbier and worn.

"That's them!" whispered Blackwater, "and the tall one's wearing my clothes!"

I had to grab Blackwater and pull him back down. "Sh-h-h-h," I said.

"Aw, he's dead and long gone. His body is probably already in Memphy," said Amos.

"I don't trust'im. He's too nice. You got to watch the nice ones. They're the ones to stab you right in the back. He may be around here somewheres." The one called Jethro began to look around the place. We all dropped our heads and stayed very quiet.

"Come here Jethro, he's long gone or dead. Git over here and less look for a drink. I hope all the liquor is still here!"

"Our guns! I don't see our guns, Amos!" Jethro was searching the keel, then the shore.

"Looky here! Jest like we left them," called Amos as he stood over the crates and barrels.

Jethro stopped scouring the woods around us and headed to the keel.

Amos had knocked the lid off one of the barrels and pulled out a jug.

"Have a drink," he said.

He handed that jug to Jethro and pulled out another one for himself. They sat and drank for what seemed to be hours. They had pulled off their boots and made themselves comfortable. We could hear talking but we could not make out what they were saying. Before long, they had drunk almost two jugs apiece and had passed out on the keel.

With their two limp bodies sprawled across the deck, the three of us eased up to the boat. As Blackwater and I gently and quietly pushed the keel off the shoreline, Cletus already knew what to do. In one swift motion, he jumped on the deck, grabbed the two by their shirt collars, and tossed them over the side nearest the middle of the river. The dousing they got in the cold river water shocked them awake. They began to thrash and splash and holler out.

"Help!"

"Save us!"

Cletus had grabbed the other pole and we both began to push the keel hard and fast into the current. The two in the water had grabbed hold of the side of the boat and they were coughing and gasping for air.

When they finally looked up, they saw their old friend, Blackwater, staring at them down the barrel of his flintlock.

"I presume you fellows never thought you would be meeting me like this, did you?"

Blackwater glared down at them.

The two men were holding on for dear life. The keel got caught in the current of the Ohio and we were being pushed along the river. We were hoping that we had pushed off hard enough and far enough to catch the drift and be carried to the calmer waters on the south side of the river. It worked, and we were now able to sink our poles in the river bottom and control our moving. We worked the poles into position in the front of the keel and we used them to slow and then stop the boat.

"Well, Reverend Blackwater, they are now yours. What will you do with them?" I was teasing the two in the water, as their scared faces looked at Blackwater.

"Maybe I should smash their knuckles with the butt of my gun and force them into the river to drown," Blackwater replied. "Or maybe I'll make their death quick and just shoot them in the head and be done with them."

By now the two in the water were frozen with fear.

"No I have a better idea, I think . . ."

"No, Mr. Blackwater, please don't kill us," pleaded Amos.

"That's right, Mr. Blackwater, you too nice of a man to want to kill us," begged Jethro.

Blackwater stared down at Jethro. "Too nice? I thought I heard you say the nice ones are the ones who will stab you in the back!"

"Oh, no, Mr. Blackwater, I didn't mean that! I was only funnin'."

"Well, maybe today, I won't be so nice," answered Blackwater. "Hand me your shirts."

"What?" they both chorused.

"I said, *give me your shirts*, before I turn *real* nice!" Blackwater lowered the gun to just inches above their heads. In the wink of an eye, they had removed their shirts and tossed them on deck.

"Now, your pants."

"Our wh . . .?" they began to argue, but Blackwater just lowered the gun even closer to their heads.

It took a few minutes of struggling - holding on with one hand and using the other to remove their pants - but they soon had them off and tossed next to their shirts.

"Maybe I should just go ahead and end their misery," Blackwater called out, as he pressed the tip of his barrel against Jethro's head.

CHAPTER 20

HEADING BACK
TOWARDS CAIRO

I was a little surprised at Blackwater's aggressiveness. For a brief moment, I actually thought he was going to pull the trigger, and so did Jethro and Amos. I watched their faces as they squeezed their eyes shut so as not to see the trigger pulled nor the flash of exploding gunpowder. If they could have closed their ears to the sound of it, too, they would have. When I looked back up at Blackwater, he glanced over to me and winked. I was relieved. I did not want to be a part of another killing.

"Bang!" he yelled real loud and the two jerked in the water. Slowly they realized there was not a shot and each looked to see if the other one was dead. When they looked up at Blackwater, he was laughing.

"All right you two. I'm going to let you live. But I warn you, if I ever see the likes of you anywhere downstream from Louisville to Natchez, I'll hunt you down and shoot you like a wild hog. Do you hear me?"

"Yes, Mr. Blackwater, sir. We hear you," they echoed together.

"Then let go."

"But, Mr. Blackwater, we'll drown!"

"Let go!" Blackwater screamed and the two let loose of the side of the keel. You could see both take deep breaths as they expected to go underwater. But, they were both flabbergasted to be able to touch bottom. While Blackwater was talking, Cletus and I had maneuvered the boat to the opposite side of the Ohio and we were almost to the bank. Quickly, they paddled themselves to the shore, dressed only in their union suits. As soon as they were out of reach, Cletus gave one powerful push and we were out into the current.

"What about our clothes?" yelled back Jethro.

Blackwater answered him, "For one thing, Mr. Jethro, they were my clothes, and for another, be glad you got your life."

As soon as we had drifted out of earshot, I said, "For a moment there, I thought you just might shoot them,"

"Couldn't do it," Blackwater stated, matter-of-factly. "The gun wasn't load-"

At that moment, he pulled the trigger and the gun fired harmlessly into the air.

The blast was so unexpected, Blackwater plopped backwards onto the deck of the keel – a look of utter shock on his face.

"I-I-I didn't realize it was loaded!" he screamed. "I could have killed those men!"

Blackwater sat there, shaking like a leaf.

"Remember," I said, "I loaded them when we went to find the poles."

"Of course!" Blackwater remembered as he slumped into the keel.

By now, we had drifted quickly downstream. Blackwater turned around and plopped down on the deck. His whole body was quivering.

"I-I-I can't believe I did that," he stuttered, still shaken from the ordeal.

"For a moment there, I wasn't too sure you were going to back off that trigger finger or not."

"No, I couldn't have shot them on purpose. I just can't believe I stood up to those two thugs. They had terrorized me from the moment we left Pittsborough. I-I, oh, my head is spinning, I . ." Blackwater's voice trailed off as his eyes rolled back into his head and he passed out.

Cletus and I looked at each other, smiled, and continued to lazily push the keel down river. When I looked downstream, I recognized we were not far from reaching Cairo. Cletus must have noticed it too. He was standing near the bow of the keel, frozen, staring straight ahead.

"Cletus!" I called. "Head for those trees." I pushed my pole deeply and tried to find leverage to guide us to the left and out of the current, but I wasn't strong enough. I looked back up at Cletus and he was still frozen in the same spot.

"Cletus!" I yelled louder. "Help me!" He slowly turned around.

"I's can'ts go back Massa Mike, I's can'ts."

"Then help me push the boat to those trees ahead. Now!"

Cletus seemed to come to his senses and I watched as he grabbed the pole and plunged it deep into the water. He must have hit ground. The keel abruptly slowed and swerved to the left, twisting the boat around. Now, my end was moving toward the shore. Cletus pulled his pole up and moved to where I was standing. Again, he drove the pole into the mud below, and again, the keel flipped ends. By this time, we were close to the bank and I could use the length of my pole to pull against the side and force us to the edge of the river. Cletus held the pole with both hands under his arm and with one more mighty push, slammed it hard into the muck, pushing the boat up onto the bank. As good a keelman as my dad had been, I am not sure he could have done what Cletus had just accomplished.

He wasn't even winded when he asked, "Now, sir, wat we's do?"

For the first time, I felt a void of ideas. It seemed like we had been running forever. I took a deep breath and sat next to where Blackwater had passed out. The only thought in my head was, *I want to go home.*

"We cans wait until dark, sir," Cletus said, trying to think for me. "Dey won't be lookin' fer us at night." He looked up at the sky. "Dis night bees clear. We's can make it."

He paused, waiting for me to respond, but I was too tired to think. "I's just don't wants to go back," he pleaded.

Cletus jumped off the keel and plopped on the bank. He sat near a h0neysuckle vine and began tugging out the nectar and licking the stem.

He was right. He would get blamed and I would be just an innocent bystander. The town would probably think I was kidnapped and held hostage against my will. Cletus would be blamed for that, too. I could tell them the truth, but they would think I had become touched in the head after such a tenuous ordeal. They would believe I was afraid to tell the truth - that Cletus had put a spell on me or I was afraid he would escape and come after me and kill me like he did the others. I knew the truth and he knew the truth, but who would believe a black man or a white boy, especially the son of the lying-est braggart ever to set toe to the Mississippi. I had no choice. I had to stay with Cletus. I wanted to make sure he was safe and we had to keep moving.

"We are not going back, Cletus. We will travel at night. As soon as night falls, we'll push on." I looked down at Blackwater. What was I going to tell him? He had lied to us but he did finally tell us the truth. Should we tell him that we had been running, living a lie ourselves? Should we tell him we were murderers? How would we explain traveling at night? Hiding? Afraid to stop in Cairo? If he knew the truth, would he turn us in the first opportunity he got? Was that a chance we wanted to take? By now the reward money could be in the hundreds; maybe a thousand dollars. Mighty tempting for a preacher who lost all his money. We would have to cross that bridge when we came to it.

Right now, I could only focus on how very hungry I was.

"Cletus, grab the guns and let's find something to eat." I knew those honeysuckles would not be very filling. I tied the boat off on a nearby tree, and we left Blackwater to his rest. I wanted to walk as deep as I could into the woods so the shots would not attract attention. It wasn't long before we saw a couple of rabbits in a thicket.

"Cletus, take aim," I whispered, my eyes set on the prey before us. I waited but no shot. I looked back and Cletus was holding the gun like it had a disease.

"Cletus, that's our meal before you. Now, lower your barrel, look down the sight and pull the trigger." I watched as he moved in slow motion. He held the gun out in front of him. "Pull the butt to your shoulder." He looked at me with a puzzled face and glanced down at his rear end. "No, not that butt, the butt of the gun!" I reached over and pulled the stock against his shoulder and directed the barrel toward his target. "When you have lined up the sight with the end of your barrel and you got a bead on your intended, take a deep breath, hold it and then, pull the . . ."

"Bam!"

Before I could say "trigger slowly," Cletus had let off a shot. The gun recoiled and Cletus dropped it and jumped back. His eyes were as big as dinner plates. I figured he completely missed his mark, but a big grin came across his face.

"I's do it, Massa Mike. I's gots us a rabbit!" I looked back into the thicket and sure enough, a rabbit laid dead.

It was a good size and it would feed the three of us handily. I handed my gun to Cletus as I walked over to pick up our dinner. When I turned around, Cletus had my gun raised, pointed directly at me.

"Cletus, what are you-?"

"Bam!" The gun rang out and it startled me so much, I fell backwards. I was so mad that he would shoot at me.

"Are you crazy! Are you trying to kill me?" I screamed at him.

Cletus didn't hear a word I was yelling. Instead, he was jumping up and down with a grin as wide as the river.

"I's gots a nudder one, Massa Mike!"

I looked a few yards away and there laid another rabbit.

"I's ain't ner shoots a gun 'fore, Massa Mike, and I's already knows how to shoot!"

Beginner's luck, I thought. But I had to admit, getting two for two *was* good shooting.

"I's a better shot 'an Mr. Blackwater, is I, Massa Mike?"

"Yes, Cletus, you are definitely better than Blackwater," I said, but then I thought, *Who wasn't?*

"Let's go show'im wat I's do." Cletus didn't wait for me. He began to head back to the boat. He left me to carry his two dead rabbits.

I didn't realize how far we had walked, so deep into the woods.

Cletus was not that far in front of me, but I noticed he had stopped up ahead. I figured he had spotted another rabbit. The only problem, he did not have a loaded gun and couldn't shoot anymore. I walked up carefully behind him and when I was near, he turned around and motioned for me to be quiet.

"Can ya hears dat?" he asked.

I stopped, straining to listen.

It was voices! Was Blackwater talking aloud to himself? Was someone talking to Blackwater? I started to walk carefully toward them. Soon, I could almost see the river, and I could hear much better now.

"What's that you say? Two young men, you say?" It was Blackwater. He was talking to someone.

CHAPTER 21

GETTING PAST CAIRO

"Sorry, I couldn't help you, gents. Haven't seen anyone to match that description."

"We think they were headed upriver, maybe going north," said a voice I did not recognize.

"No," answered Blackwater, "I can't say I've seen a living soul since I left Pittsborough."

"Well, sir, it seems we have word that you spoke with a local trapper by the name of Coppersmith. Did you not?"

"Oh, yes, as a matter of fact I did. I had forgotten. Just a brief encounter. I hardly thought it mattered."

I could tell by Blackwater's voice he was not used to lying.

"He says he sent a rather large black boy and puny little white fella to you. Are you saying they never showed up?"

Puny? He called me puny? I muttered under my breath.

"Why, of course, that is exactly what I am saying. I am a preacher of the Word of God. Why would I have a reason to lie, my good man?"

"Sorry, Reverend, my aim is not to doubt you. We are just trying to find those two. Beggin' your pardon, we'll leave you be. But if you do run across those two, on your travels south, you'll let someone know, won't you?"

"As a man of God, I would be obliged to do so. Good day, gentlemen."

"Good day, Reverend."

I could hear the lapping of waves and the clunk of poles banging against the side of a keel. Cletus and I waited until we were sure the boat was out of ear shot and view before we crept back to Blackwater and his boat.

When Blackwater saw us emerge from the woods, he glanced around and said to us sternly, "I think you two owe me an explanation. I was making falsehoods about you!" He looked heaven-ward and moaned, "God forgive me!"

I knew we had to tell the truth, but I wanted to know first what they told Blackwater.

"What did those men want?" I questioned.

"They wanted you two, that's what!"

"Did they tell you why they wanted us?"

"I presume they *wanted* you because you are *wanted* men! And now I am a liar!"

Blackwater dropped to his knees on the deck, shaking his head in disbelief. He put his hands together and began to pray, "Dear Lord, please forgive me! I have sinned and I need Your forgiveness! Please, Lord!" Then he glared at us and continued, "I trusted you two! You lied to me!"

Now I stopped feeling worried and began to feel defiant.

"Now, just a minute, Mr. Blackwater!"

"Reverend," Cletus interjected.

"Reverend," I added. "I seem to remember a tale you told that was not exactly the truth." I looked over at Cletus, trying to decide how much of the truth I needed to tell Blackwater about us.

I continued. "You are right, Reverend Blackwater, we didn't tell you the whole truth. It just never came up."

"Now I found myself lying again, *for you!*" Blackwater continued explaining to us. "I preach against lying and liars and here I was staring another man in the eye and telling him I never saw you two before! I dare say that does not reflect well on my ministry!" Blackwater slumped, muttering to himself. "Oh, God please, please forgive me for lying. Thank you, Jesus!"

"Would it make a difference if we told you we are innocent? That we never intentionally harmed a living soul? That what we did was to protect our lives and," I stopped. Somehow, I didn't feel like any explanation would matter to Blackwater.

There was a long period of quiet when no one could think of a thing to say. Cletus sat down and began to snap off honeysuckles again. I was gazing across the river towards home, and Blackwater had removed his shoes and he was rubbing his feet.

"Look," Blackwater said as he broke the silence, "I owe you two. You saved my life back there with those two cutthroats. When I first met you, I knew something was amiss, otherwise why would you be out here? I lied to protect you and I've asked God to forgive me. My prayer is that it was for the right cause."

"I can assure you Mr. Blackwater, you did the right thing," I replied.

"You believed me so I will believe you, fair enough?" asked Blackwater.

"Dat's mightily fair, Rev'rend Blackwater. Ya is a good man o' God," chimed in Cletus.

Blackwater sighed deeply, wiped his face with the palms of his hands, then slapped his palms on his knees. "All right, boys, what next? I am sure you two cannot stay here very long."

"No, sir, we can't. Cletus and I want to get to Memphis. That is, if you will allow us to travel along with you."

"It would be my pleasure."

The mood on the boat got a lot less tense when Cletus lightened up the situation with his announcement.

"I's gots us sum food, Rev'end Blackwater. I's shot'em mysef. Two rabbits. Fi'st time, too." Cletus had grabbed the two rabbits out of my hand and held the bloody game right in front of Blackwater's face. "See?" he added.

Blackwater turned his head away and covered his mouth to keep from gagging. "That's wonderful, Cletus. I'm sure they will cook up nicely."

"Cletus, why don't you let me skin and gut them, and you work on the fire. Reverend, could you gather some firewood?"

Blackwater turned away from the spot Cletus had laid the rabbits for me to skin, and quickly headed off to pick up wood for the fire.

Cletus was so proud of the kill he had made. He seemed to forget for a moment the trouble he was in. As I assembled a few twigs and leaves together to light the kindling, I heard Cletus humming a tune. I did not recognize it. It sounded deep and soulful. I decided I shouldn't ask him about it. He seemed so content for the first time since I had met him.

I had never noticed it before, but Cletus had a knife. It was a small pocketknife, black, with just one small blade. As I watched him cut a branch with it for a spit, I could see the initials, "EM", carved into the handle. *Who was EM?* I thought. Maybe it belonged to Mr. Morten. I never knew his first name. If Cletus was caught with that knife on him, everyone would believe he stole it. Slaves weren't supposed to have knives. I'm sure Mr. Morten would have given it to him, but who would believe it now? I started to ask Cletus about the knife, but Blackwater interrupted me.

"Is this enough wood?"

His arms were so loaded down, you couldn't see his upper body.

"Oh yes, that will be enough to last us all night," I answered.

The whole time I had been working on the rabbits, I kept an eye out on the river. I would not be surprised if the boat out looking for us would turn around and backtrack this way again.

While I was deep in thought, Cletus had finished the fire. He took both rabbits and put them on the spit over the fire. In a moment, the smell of cooked meat filled our noses. Our mouths began to water very quickly.

The rest of the night, we sat around the fire and Blackwater began to tell us stories from the Bible. He told us that we reminded him of two friends in the Bible - David and Jonathan. He said they helped each other, just like we were doing. Blackwater said they weren't brothers but they acted like brothers, the same way we acted like brothers. I never thought of Cletus as a brother. I had brothers, but they were younger, and I never considered them as friends. Cletus was definitely my friend, and if that friendship made us act like brothers, then so be it.

If we ever got through this and the truth was known, I was sure of one thing - we would be more than just friends. I think brothers we would be.

I fell asleep that night listening to Blackwater singing hymns and to Cletus singing his own spirituals. However, my calm slumber was rudely interrupted when I heard Blackwater's voice.

"They're back!"

Back? Who's back? I said to myself.

CHAPTER 22

AVOIDING THE LAW

I rolled over to the flat of my stomach and peered up. I didn't see anything. My eyes were still foggy from the night's sleep, but I could hear Cletus and Blackwater moving in the dim light of morning. I heard Cletus whisper again, "Dey's back."

I felt the keel being pushed out into the water, and it rocked back and forth. I heard Cletus grunting as he shoved the boat off the shore with all his might; and then I heard water lapping against the sides. I rubbed my eyes and I looked up to see Cletus jumping onto the deck. Even Blackwater had a pole and was ramming it hard against the bank, forcing the keel away from the shore.

"Who's back?" I asked aloud.

"Sh-h-h-h!" was the response I got from both of them.

I eased up in a sitting position and tried to see what was happening. Cletus was frantically pushing the keel and I was surprised at the speed and the quiet of his work. Blackwater was at the back of the boat, working to steer it into the strong current. As my eyes began to adjust to the hazy light of an early morning fog, I strained to see what was happening. I still could not see anything, but then I heard voices coming across the water. They were indistinct, but seemed to be getting louder. At first, I thought it was coming from a long distance away, but then again, maybe not.

"What's going on?" I demanded.

"It's them! They found us!" Blackwater muttered through clenched teeth.

"Which them?" I pleaded. "Them from last night, or them from yesterday morning?"

"Yes!" he answered back.

"Yes?" I felt confused and still a little groggy from my rude awakening.

"Yes, it's the men from yesterday who were asking about you, and my two 'unfriendly' friends are with them!" Blackwater answered.

"Are you sure?" I asked.

"Do you want to wait around and find out?" replied Blackwater.

He was right. Now was not the time to question. We didn't need them to stumble on us again. I was now awake and very alert. I grabbed for Blackwater's pole and he was more than happy to give it to me. I joined Cletus in pushing us out into the midstream. I didn't need to do much. Cletus had worked hard to get us moving fast and in the right direction. It was still not very light out but the approaching dawn began to filter through the trees. I noticed the voices began to fade and I could tell we were making better time. The distance between us and the boat behind was growing.

In the distance across the still water of the Ohio, I could see the approaching shores of Cairo. I could just barely make out the piers and the docks jutting out into the river and just beyond them would be the Mississippi. As we drew closer we saw the Morten paddlewheel – the <u>Cairo Queen</u>; still in the same place we last saw it. I looked at Cletus. He had pulled his pole up out of the water and stood straight up to gaze at his former home. I looked up the bank and I could see the shadowy forms of the buildings and stores and homes I had passed many times. In the silence and stillness of daybreak, we floated past. In a moment, I was overcome by sadness. My mom and my brothers, my home, - I wanted to see them terribly. But in my heart, I knew I could never go home again. Not a sound was made as we swiftly soared over the glassy, early morning waters, barely making a ripple. Cairo was now in our past, and the Mississippi was about to carry us to our future.

"Let's don't stop now, boys. I think we have lost them, but you can never be too certain." Blackwater's voice snapped us out of our daydreaming, and we again began to pole down the river.

"What happened back there?" I asked again. This time I was hoping for a better answer.

"Obviously, the men who stopped by yesterday looking for you, continued up river and ran into Jethro and Amos. I am sure they told them everything," Blackwater explained. "They found out I lied about knowing you, and I am sure they were coming back to get the both of you and get me."

"But you don't know that for sure," I said.

"I recognized the voices," said Blackwater, "I will never forget those two hooligans for as long as I live."

"And da keel was da same as dose men who was lookin' fer us," said Cletus.

"And you know that?" I asked Cletus. "How?"

"The poles hittin' the side of the boat, the rhythm of the keelmen as they poled." I couldn't believe what Cletus was telling me. He continued. "It's da sound, Massa Mike. Dat's my music. Dat's wat I's knows and dat's wat I's feels. I's knewed it was dem."

I sighed and didn't try to figure it out. "Well, we seem to have lost them for now. Staying in the main current will keep us way ahead of them. Mr. Blackwater, are you ready to head for Memphis?"

"Oh, yes!" He turned to me and smiled. "Now that we appear to be a safe distance ahead, may I give it a go?" He reached his hand out for my pole and I handed it to him. He gripped it tightly and lowered it slowly into the water.

"Ne'er taut ya bees a riberman, is dat true, Mr. Blackwater?" Cletus asked.

"There are a lot of things I have learned on this trip," he answered, "and a lot more I need to absorb."

CHAPTER 23

EVERYONE HAS A QUESTION

Soon, we had settled into the rhythm of the ride and we all stopped talking. We had finally arrived at a place where I, nor Blackwater, had ever been. I watched as the rugged shore line began to melt into the edge of the river. I was surprised to see the number of trees growing in the water. Or maybe the water was high and had flooded them. I had heard of floods, and Cairo had had its share of high water, but now the river seemed to spread out and widen far into the landscape. The swift movement of the keel offered a brisk breeze in our faces, and the smooth current made me feel like I was floating on clouds.

We had watched the sun rise to our left and drift quickly across the sky and settle behind trees on the western bank. Flicks of shadows from the taller trees flashed across our eyes. Cletus seemed tireless as he continued to pole us along the river. Blackwater would pause every now and then, and take in all that the nature around us had to offer. I had become content to just sit on the deck, leaning against some of the barrels.

"I's hungry!" Cletus broke the silence with a bellow.

"Good point, Cletus," agreed Blackwater, "I could do with a hearty meal."

"I couldn't agree more," I chimed in, "We better shore for the night and find something to eat before we lose all of our light."

Cletus turned us into a clearing between several large cypress trees where the bank seemed dry and stable.

"Game!" yelled out Blackwater, "We need to have game."

"Well," I sighed, stretching from the hours I spend lazing on the keel, "I guess I need to earn my keep." I grabbed the rifle and leaped to the bank just as Cletus hit bottom. "You two start the fire and I will find the food."

I walked directly east with the sun at my back, still barely filtering in the tree branches overhead. I had only been walking about thirty minutes when I heard the blast of a musket.

Fear gripped me as my mind raced back to the keel with Blackwater and Cletus. *Had the men caught up to us? Had river pirates attacked? Is someone hurt?*

I raced back, following the fading glimpses of light in the limbs overhead, trying hard not to make a sound. But there were sounds. Loud sounds. Men talking. Boisterous talking. I slowed my pace and turned my ear to the noise. It was Cletus and Blackwater, and they were laughing!

I sighed and knew everything must be all right. I could soon see the bright flames of a fire and when I saw they were having a grand old time, I became angry.

"I was trying to find us something to eat!" I said angrily. "Shooting off your gun probably scared off any animal within a mile of us. Now, what are we. . ." I stopped in mid-sentence when I saw Cletus turn around from skinning the second biggest buck I had ever seen.

"Where did you get that? Cletus, you bagged a beauty!"

He laughed, "Not me. Reverend Blackwater gots dis one."

"Can you believe it, Young Mike?" Blackwater beamed. "You hadn't been gone long and wonder of wonders, this deer just meandered right into the clearing. The sunlight behind us must have blinded him. He didn't move. Cletus reached for the other gun and instead of shooting it himself, he handed the blasted thing to me!"

"I's figures dis be one more tang he needs to learn," added Cletus.

"Well, I couldn't have done it by myself," continued Blackwater, "Cletus steadied the gun for me and whispered instructions to me – 'cradle the barrel, place the butt against my shoulder, hold my breath, slowly squeeze the trigger.'

"When the darn thing went off, it almost landed me on my rear-end!"

"And he gots'm," grinned Cletus.

"And I got'm," Blackwater mimicked, grinning even bigger.

We had a great feast that night. For the first time, we all seemed to feel relaxed, and we laughed at the retelling of Blackwater's hunting success several times over during the evening. As the venison began to settle in our stomachs, a quiet calm came over us as we stared into the dying embers of the fire.

I finally broke the silence. "I have a question. Cletus, that was mighty noble of you to let Mr. Blackwater shoot, knowing what an awful shot he had been when we first met. Why didn't you shoot?"

"Massa Mike, I's don't like guns, ne'er had. Dey scars me."

"But, you told me exactly what to do," Blackwater remarked.

"Oh, I's 'members wat ya tells me 'afore - talkin' about shootin'. I just 'membered wat ya says and I tells Massa Blackwater da same tang."

It was quiet again for a moment before Blackwater spoke up. "Now, I have a question. You don't have to tell me an answer, unless you want to. It makes no never mind to me. But if you want to get it off your chests, I am here to listen, not to judge. God takes care of the judging and I take care of the listening," then he added, "and the praying."

He paused, looking at both of us, to see if he should continue. I glanced at Cletus and we seemed to know where Blackwater was going. Cletus didn't seem to object, so I just let Blackwater continue.

"You boys have been running from something or someone, I know that. I gather by your anxiousness to run that it must be somewhat serious. I believe a man is not guilty until all the facts are in. I am not sure what the facts are in your circumstance, but if you want to share your story with me, I'll listen. You boys have not given me a reason to doubt your sincerity. You have been fair with me and have respected me. I somehow doubt that the trouble you're in is as bad as you think it is. I won't think any less of you one way or the other, no matter what happened."

Blackwater stopped. He gave us opportunity to tell our story. Finally, I felt a yearning to tell someone what happened; to tell the truth.

Before I could barely get my mouth around a word, Cletus blurted out, "I's runs away from my Massa."

Blackwater shifted his body, "Well, that is pretty serious, no doubt," he said, "Was there a reason?"

"He was getting beat up mighty awful," I interrupted, trying to think fast on my feet, "If I hadn't got Cletus away, that man would have killed him." I couldn't believe Cletus was lyin' and I was going right along with it; and to a preacher, no less.

"You mean you are involved because you helped him escape, right? Anyone else involved in this?"

"No," I moaned. "We're both going to be blamed. If we hadn't run, Cletus would be dead by now."

"I am sure running sounded good at the time," agreed Blackwater, "But if you were innocent, couldn't you have stayed and told the authorities?"

"Not once a black man runs," added Cletus, "White peoples don't takes kindly to slaves runnin' away."

"Well, it sounds like you boys are between a rock and hard place," Blackwater said, "I believe your story. I trust you. You saved me from sure death, and I owe you. I understand your plight. You don't have to say anymore. I won't mention it again." Blackwater leaned back on the ground and fell right to sleep.

Cletus and I were still awake. Both of us knew we had lied through our teeth, and lied big time to a man of the cloth – a man who had been very honest with us. This was the most we had talked about what happened. As I stared off into the darkness, it was Cletus' turn to break the silence. "Now, I has a question."

"What is it Cletus?"

"Doze the riber e'er end?"

"What do you mean?"

"I's means, I's sees the riber and it's always movin', never stoppin'. Doze it ever end?"

"Yea, Cletus, it does end; just south of New Orleans, it empties into the Gulf of Mexico. Yea, it does end. How could you not know that?"

"I's too 'fraid to asks and I's ne'er learned it from my Mamma. I's ne'er taut 'bout it 'til I's gots on the riber mysef." Cletus smiled broadly. "Dat's good, Massa Mike, dat's real good."

"Why do you ask?"

"Well, I's figures my runnin' was likes da riber runnin' and neber endin'. But ya says da riber doze end, so maybe my runnin' will end one day, too."

"Yea, you're right, Cletus, it will all end one day, just like the river."

Cletus nodded and he too rolled over and fell fast asleep.

The fire had burned to only a few red coals and the coolness of the night gave me a chill. I pushed a few logs into the middle of the embers and watched as the growing flames gave rise to a warming heat. It would still be burning when we got up in the morning, I hoped. I tried to sleep myself, but the words of Cletus kept repeating in my mind. *Does the river ever end? Will my running ever end?* I kept hearing it over and over again. I may have convinced Cletus, but when I thought about my own life, I wasn't so sure.

I woke up to the singing of hymns and spirituals by Cletus and Blackwater. Both sounded more chipper than I have ever heard them before. The smell of venison filled my nostrils, and I jumped up hungry, looking for some of the meat.

Blackwater saw me and said, "We planned to eat as soon as we were safely underway. Cletus has put the rest of the game on the boat."

Without saying a word, I shuffled to the boat as Cletus put out the fire.

"We definitely don't need anyone following our trail," bellowed Cletus with confidence in his voice and with words that belied his lack of schooling. "That would be disastrous, right, Reverend?"

"You are absolutely correct, my man!" answered Blackwater.

I stood there for a moment. *Did I just hear how Cletus was talking?*

"Cletus," I said in amazement after hearing him speak. "Y-Your voice – it's different, it's – Cletus you sound so different!"

"What a story, Mike," interjected Blackwater. "An amazing story if I ever heard one!"

Cletus smiled shyly. "I'll explain it all to you later, Mike."

"Let's go boys," Blackwater called, "Memphis is calling!"

I was still standing on the boat, amazed at how Cletus was talking as we pushed out into the river.

Then Cletus began again, "We were talking this morning, Mike, and we named our boat. We're calling it <u>God's Freedom Queen</u>."

"And we decided that Mr. Blackwater is the captain of our boat and you are the foreman." Cletus sheepishly added, "If that's okay with you."

I was still amazed at the words and sound coming out of Cletus' mouth. He sounded so different, so learned. His voice, his speech, his words had changed so much – and overnight!

Cletus interrupted my state of shock. "Well, Foreman, Mr. Mike, are you content with that?"

I smiled and said, "Uh, what? Oh, why, Cletus, I think you should be foreman. Don't you think, Mr. Blackwater, or Reverend, or, I mean Captain Blackwater?"

"Why, that is a noble turn, Mr. Fink. I concur! Foreman Cletus! Sail this magnificent ship on to Memphis!"

Cletus seemed to glow, "Yes, Captain, to Memphis we sail."

He was taking great pride in his new-found role and he seemed to pole even harder than before, but then he stopped and turned to me.

"But you, Mr. Mike, who are you?"

"Me?" I thought, "Why, every great vessel of the sea has passengers. I'll be your passenger. Fair enough?"

"Yes, sir, Mr. Mike, a passenger you will be!" With that, Cletus puffed out his chest and pushed <u>God's Freedom Queen</u> on toward Memphis.

"Onward to Memphis, Odysseus! Onward to Memphis!" shouted Blackwater.

Odysseus? Who is he calling Odysseus?

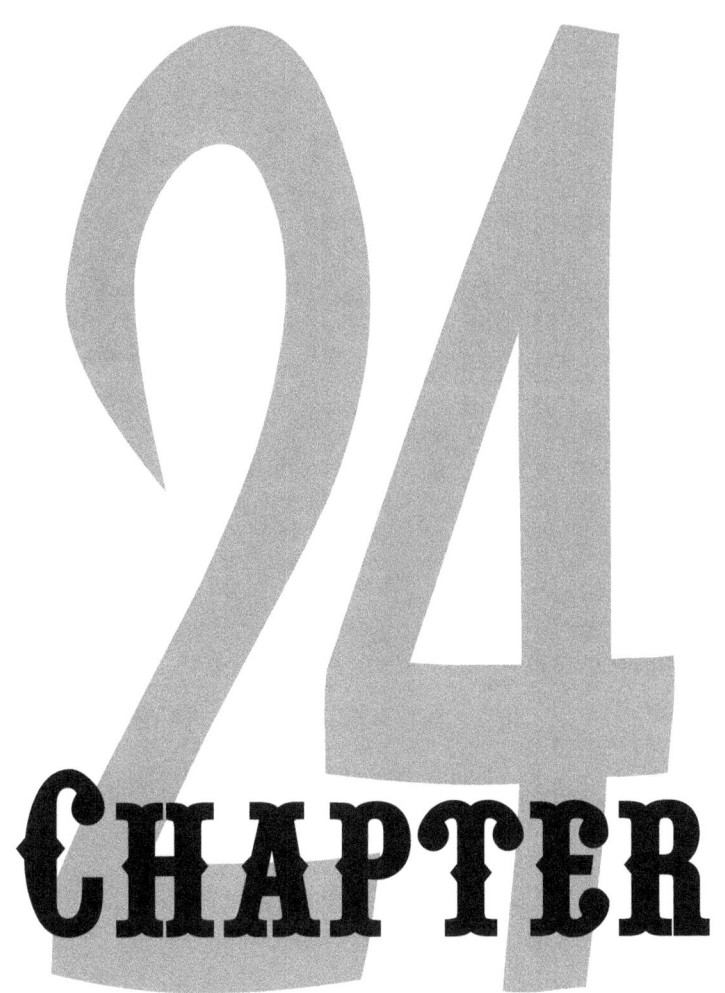

CHAPTER 24

TALES OF THE
MIGHTY MISSISSIPPI

I had heard tales about how the Mississippi would widen as you traveled south. It would get so wide, I was told, that you could not hear a person holler from one bank to the other. Now that the Ohio and Mississippi ran together, it seemed to be wider already. The river pilots on the Mississippi talked about the upper Mississippi from Cairo, north, past St. Louis. They talked about how much straighter the river was, with bluffs and rocky shores and cliffs holding back the river. I had heard how fast you would travel heading downstream and how difficult it was to move upstream, at least until the paddlewheels came. In the upper Mississippi, the banks were higher, harder and rockier and there was not as much flooding. Oh, it would flood, but as the river moved south, the banks would overflow almost every year.

Here, the lower Mississippi started and went south to New Orleans, and out into the Gulf of Mexico. The banks were lower, softer and wider. The river would twist and turn, and sometimes it would split and make huge ox bows, not knowing which way it wanted to go. Sometimes boat captains from the upper Mississippi would travel down to Cairo to get a look at the river, to see what changes to expect. They would come back with tales of how the river would completely change direction. Instead of going right, it would go left, and sometimes the river would cut right through the land and make a new path. All these changes in the river made travel on the lower Mississippi somewhat treacherous.

Sometimes a captain would come to a split, and if he picked the wrong way, he could end up in a slough, and would have to backtrack to get out. Sometimes they would have to be dragged out. Not only was the lower Mississippi difficult to navigate, it was prone to vicious flooding. I heard tell that every town from Cairo south on the lower Mississippi flooded, at one time or the other. Now, maybe they didn't flood every year, but sometimes they would flood one year and then flood the next, and then they wouldn't flood for five or six years. Some years the water dropped so low, a body could almost walk across it from Illinois to Missouri.

Somewhere near here was San Madrid; the place my mom feared as much as the Mississippi, the Ohio, and Indians all put together. Right now, it seemed calm and peaceful like. She told me many times about the earthquake that started here; how it kept on, for a year, shaking and rattling. She told me how the river would swallow up a forest or a field in one place and then belch up land in another. She said the river at times would flow backwards and how it would leave lakes where there once was only dry land and leave islands where once there was only the river.

I used to hear many other tales about the river from my dad, from the travelers who would stop in Cairo, and from Mr. Morten. Mr. Morten. I hadn't had much time to think about him or what had happened in Cairo that night. How long ago was it? Two nights? Three nights? Four or five? Seemed like it had been forever. After all the traveling we had done, we were now just a day from where it all happened. My thoughts about the river and what had happened to Cletus and me were interrupted by Blackwater.

"This river is different," Blackwater sounded very cautious. "Something doesn't feel right. Be careful, boys."

My daydreaming was over.

I looked around. I didn't understand what Blackwater was talking about. Everything seemed fine to me. At least, until I looked at Cletus. He looked nervous. *What was happening? Should I be afraid?*

I looked up and saw the sky. It was quickly becoming as black as the coal from the hills of Carbondale.

Suddenly the rain began to fall.

25

CHAPTER

STORM ON THE RIVER

At first it was just a sprinkle, but then in a flash of lightning, it was falling harder and the wind lashed at my face. *How had the wind and rain picked up this hard this fast?* I asked myself. My clothes were now drenched, and the pouring rain was making it hard to see much past the front of our boat. I had remembered the shore being only a few yards away, but now I could not see it.

It was going to be a storm like I had never seen before.

Blackwater was staring up ahead. "A storm? Oh, I feel we are more than ready for a storm, and I hope it doesn't delay our plans."

I turned to look up ahead at what just moments before seemed like a clear day far to the south, but now had turned into a streak of sky - dark with rain-heavy clouds.

Up to this point, the river had been smooth with little or no waves at most. Now, downstream the river looked choppy with waves splashing in all directions. I could see the trees on either shore bending in all directions with the tree tops swaying in the swirling, thunderous skies. The force of the river was making it difficult to move our keel downstream. For the second time in my life, the thought of dying entered my mind. In the blink of an eye, the storm was upon us.

"Might be a rough ride, but we can't afford to stop, not with the prospect of anyone following us. Keep going, Mister Blackwater?" I asked.

"Let's go for it, boys."

"No stopping now, Mister Mike," said Cletus.

"Mister Blackwater, you may be in danger of losing some or all of your cargo. You still want to fight the storm?" I asked again.

"Well, it's not the cargo I thought it was anyway. If I lose it, I lose it."

"All right, everyone. Be ready to hang on."

The rain and the wind had picked up even more. It was coming down hard now, and the drops stung our faces. With the storm coming up the river, it would be difficult to judge the currents and the waves would be erratic and wild, making it hard to steer.

With a tempest before us and the possibility of a boatload of angry men behind us, we pressed on. Either way we could lose our lives.

This was not a storm we were prepared for. Before we knew what was happening, we had lost control of our boat. Cletus had been working extra hard to keep us upright and moving in the right direction. But with the wind blowing and the rain pelting us painfully, it felt like sharp smacks against our skin. Either the river began to widen, or else we could not see either bank. With the water churning, we could not tell upstream from downstream. At times, I felt we were going in circles.

"I hear voices, Mike," Cletus screamed out to me. "It's men! I hear them yelling!"

I could see his head moving left to right and back to left again, straining to find its origin.

"It's over there!" he hollered, pointing to the left.

Instinctively, he began to pull the boat toward the sound, or where he thought the sound was coming from. I still couldn't hear anything but the sheets of rain that were filling the boat with water. I tried to push the boat along with Cletus. Soon I could hear voices too and they sounded like men. *Men? Are they looking for us? Should we be afraid?* In the midst of the storm, we could not tell from which direction the voices were coming, and our eyes were blinded by the searing rain. I watched Cletus as he strained to locate the direction of the voices.

"This way," he commanded.

I looked ahead of us and I could see arms and heads thrashing in the water, clinging to limbs and tree trunks. I tried to keep the boat steady as Cletus reached into the water and lifted man after man into the boat. Each one collapsed onto the deck, breathing heavy and coughing up river water.

Blackwater and I kept pushing us to shore, and once we hit land the men started crawling off. He and I helped the men up the bank and away from the water.

"You got to save Davey!" one of them gasped, "We think he's, he's crashed on a bar in the middle!"

Cletus glanced around, wiping the rain water from his face, but it kept pouring across his eyes. "I can hear him!" he shouted. Without hesitation, he pushed off. In a few blinks of the eye, he had disappeared in the cloud of fog and rain. As we tended to the men, I looked back over the river. *I hope he knows what he is doing,* I said to myself. *I hope he comes back alive.*

CHAPTER 26

WHO WERE THESE MEN?

The storm continued to pelt us with the rain and wind. We huddled up on the shore with the men that had been rescued. We had all been coughing and breathing heavy from the struggle we had just endured. After a long silence, they began to talk.

"That's a brave young man, you got there," one of the men said to me. "Is he yours?"

I glanced at him, not sure by what he meant. Then I realized he thought Cletus was a slave. I had almost forgot myself.

"Oh, he's not mine," I replied. "Reckon he don't belong to anyone anymore."

"A freed slave, huh?"

"Yea, freed." I was hoping he would not ask me how.

The men looked strange, for rivermen. They wore heavy boots and oversized coats - too bulky for someone moving down the river. Their hands showed new blisters with raw spots that were oozing blood. They looked cold, like fish out of water. They laid on the bank gasping for breath, appearing more like drowning rats saved at the last minute.

"What happened out there?" asked Blackwater, trying to make conversation and break the spell of silence.

"Davey's skiff hit a tree stump in the storm, cracked a plank and sprung a leak. He was helpin' his men from his boat to ours. He was down in the hole, and the hatchway collapsed when a huge tree fell on it. He was the last one, then his boat hit a sandbar and broke up. We tried to turn around, but the extra men and rain started to swamp us."

"We got caught up in a whirlpool," another added, "and it spun us around so many times, our heads were swimmin'."

"Look. We ain't boatsmen. Davey thought we could turn a dollar by takin' goods to market in Memphis or maybe all the way to New Orleans."

"Now it looks like Davey is gone."

It got quiet for a minute and then Blackwater spoke up again.

"Uh, this Davey you speak about - that wouldn't be the famous Colonel Davey Crockett, the Congressman and woodsman, would it."

"One'n the same feller," the talkative one answered.

"Davey Crockett?" Blackwater whispered to himself as he joined the rest of us with our eyes glued to the spot we last saw Cletus disappear in the driving rain. "Davey Crockett?" he whispered again.

CHAPTER 27

CLETUS THE RESCUER

No sooner had Blackwater mentioned the name, 'Davey Crockett' than we heard someone yell out our names.

"Blackwater! Mike! Help me!" It was Cletus, and it was coming from the river.

In a flash, Blackwater, myself and all the other men on shore ran to where we had heard the voice. Cletus was sprawled across the bank, the waves splashing up and over his body. He was lying on his back with his hand raised, holding a rope in his grip.

"Take this and pull!" he choked. "I hope he's still alive!"

Immediately the men grabbed the rope and began pulling with all their might. Blackwater and I tried to pull Cletus further up on the bank and out of the water. We couldn't do it.

"Could someone help us, please?" cried out Blackwater. Two of the men quickly came. With two of us on each arm, we were able to lift Cletus out of the water and up on the shore safely.

Behind us, we heard someone scream. "Is it the Colonel?"

There was a lot of hollering and screaming and running around as the body of another man was pulled up on the ridge of the shore.

"Yes, it's Davey!" We heard several call out, "He ain't dead, is he?"

"Get the rope off!"

"Somebody squeeze the water out of 'im!"

"Stand back, let 'im get some air!"

With everyone still yelling out instructions and hovering over the seemingly lifeless body, we could not see what was happening. Suddenly, we heard someone start coughing and then all the men let out a yell.

"He's alive!"

"He's gonna be fine!"

"Davey's alive!"

As we stood there, watching the men celebrate their joy, we had almost forgot about Cletus. I looked down and Cletus was still lying flat on his back.

"Are you all right, Cletus?" I asked.

"Yes," he answered through deep sighs. "I'm fine."

As I collected my thoughts, I said to Cletus, "Cletus, you saved his life! How did you do that? Did you swim?"

"I found a log to hold on to and I paddled as hard as I could. I didn't think I could do it, but I did! I did it, Mike. I did it!"

"Yes, Cletus, and you saved a life." Blackwater was now standing with me, looking down at Cletus. "You saved the life of Davey Crockett!"

By this time, several of the men had left the rescued Crockett and approached Cletus.

"You did a mighty fine thing there, boy," said one of them.

"You risked your own life for another, and none of us are likely to forget what you did, 'specially Davey," spoke up another.

The men reached down and tried to help Cletus up, but he waved them off and got up on his own.

"Boys, bring 'im here. Davey wants to meet the man who saved his life," we heard someone call.

Davey Crockett was now lifted up and had his arms wrapped around the shoulders of two of his friends; one on either side of him.

Cletus was now standing and facing the man he had just pulled from certain death.

"You saved my life son, for which I am mighty grateful, and I owe you more than I could ever repay. Is there anything I can do for you?" asked Crockett.

"I would be much obliged to shake your hand, man-to-man, sir," responded Cletus.

"Then a shake it will be," answered the Congressman, as he took his right arm off his friend and reached out his hand.

Cletus grinned broadly and he too reached out to take Crockett's hand. Both shook hands for a good minute. The smiles on both of their faces got everyone smiling and soon there was jovial laughter all around. Without anyone realizing it, the wind and rain had stopped just as fast as it had started.

We looked around and realized the storm that had shattered our dreams just moments before was now gone, leaving plenty of evidence in its wake.

CHAPTER 28

THE STORM WAS OVER

Everything was in disarray. Many of the kegs of liquor were broken open and most of the jugs inside were smashed. Even if the Reverend wanted to sell them, they were of no value now. Our raft was now punctured with holes and would need a lot of repair. Mister Crockett's goods didn't seem much different from ours. A few things appeared to be salvageable, but it would take all the lumber from all the boats to put together one good boat. The good news was that no lives were lost.

Cletus, the Reverend and I seemed to be in a daze as we looked at the splintered timber that used to be our boat, and the broken barrels of liquor strewed across the bank, probably two hundred yards on either side of us, up and down the river. Mingled in were the goods Mr. Crockett and his crew had planned to sell downstream in Memphis. We stood watching him and his crew as they gathered around a fire they had started with some of the wood from the boats. They seemed in much better spirits than we did. They seemed almost jovial but we were just standing stone faced in silence.

"Davey, I don't want to be the one that says 'I told ya so', but..." one of his crew said; a burly man with so much facial hair, you couldn't see his mouth or his eyes.

"This here outin' seemed doomed from the start," said another as he poked among the embers.

"What's he tryin' to say, Davey, is, we ain't boatmen. We're hunters, farmers, trappers..."

"And you're a politician!" whipped another one.

With that, they all began to laugh. Mister Crockett looked around at the debris on the shore and the lumber stuck in the cypress trees in the water. He looked back at his men, "But we lost everything we had men. There ain't hardly enough here to come close to sellin' and breakin' even."

"But, Davey, we are all alive," said the burly one.

"We're with you, Davey. We can try our chances down the river again, or we can head back home. If me and the boys had our druthers, we'd just as soon be headin' home," said one as he stood up.

We were still standing just outside the circle from his men, not making a sound.

"Well, boys," Crockett said, "I guess this was not to be."

Someone had miraculously saved Davey's gun and held it out to Davey. He grabbed it and began to wipe the mud off the barrel. Without looking up, he continued, "I hear they are offerin' four bits a pelt up in Cincy."

With that, there was a big roar and a smile shot across the Colonel's face. The men got up and started to gather as much of their personal belongings as they could find.

"There's some stuff still sellable, Davey. Are we just gonna leave it here?"

For the first time, Crockett turned to look at us, and the rest of his party followed his eyes.

Crockett glanced at us and turned back to his crew. "You know, boys, had it not been for these fellers here, we might have been driftin' face down all the way to Natchez."

He turned and looked at each one of us. "You boys saved our lives, and we could never thank you enough."

He turned back to his men and said, "Whatya say gents? Let's just give'm whatever they can gather."

"Sure."

"Give it to 'em."

"Why not. We're headin' home."

As the men filed into the woods, heading east back unto Tennessee, Crockett walked toward us. "I know you ain't got much left, and your boat ain't much more'n firewood, but whatever we had including our boats, it's yours to have, and hopefully you can glean enough to getcha where you're goin' and a few bucks in your pocket." With that, he offered his hand and we each shook it. When he got to Cletus, he put his arm around him and gave Cletus a real bear hug. Then he nodded, turned and was soon out of sight amongst the trees. We stood and looked around, surveying our loss, not feeling we had been given much of a deal. At least we were alive and we were glad of that.

"Preacher, why don't you start gathering the viable merchandise and Cletus and I will start working on gettin' a boat to put it in."

The preacher nodded and was soon hauling whatever he could find salvageable to a dry spot near where our boat had grounded. Cletus and I had the boat turned over to evaluate the damage. The only serious damage seemed to be a rather large hole near the stern, made by a Cyprus knee the boat had landed on. Even though it didn't seem that big, we had nothing to repair it with. The rudder was completed gone as well as our cabin area. "We can't repair it, can we Mister Mike?"

"Don't seem possible. We'll have to find some other way to keep going." Then we heard the preacher yell out.

"Come here boys! Hurry!"

We first thought he was in trouble, like maybe a wild beast achin' to tear him apart. We ran as fast as we could to him.

CHAPTER 29

THINGS ARE LOOKING UP

There Blackwater was, sitting on one of Crockett's skiffs.

"There isn't anything wrong with this one!"

He was right. The bottom showed no holes and the rudder seemed in good shape.

"I couldn't turn it over, but it might be better than ours."

The three of us lifted on one side and rolled the boat over. With Cletus in the middle, he handled most of the weight. Once turned over, we couldn't believe our eyes. A full shipment from one of Crockett's boats - still in barrels; still not broken. We stood for a moment to survey our good fortune.

"Hey, these are marked 'blankets'. These are marked 'cider'. Here are 'pickled eggs'."

The preacher rattled off the contents as he inspected each barrel.

"I can't believe they walked away from this. I guess they were so happy to be alive, they couldn't care less about searching for their cargo. Come on, let's keep looking. I feel much better selling these goods than all that liquor we had before."

The preacher stopped. "Of course, all of this belongs to each of us to share whatever we can get. You know 50-50-50 like."

"You mean about thirty-tree percent each, right, Reverend Blackwater?" added Cletus.

"Huh?" we both asked at the same time.

"How would you know that?" I inquired.

"Uh, a lucky guess, Mister Mike?" he answered.

"I don't think so. You are much smarter than I ever imagined."

The boat was soon loaded with all we could find. We had also found gingham cloth, moccasins, leather pouches and fur skin caps as well as a barrel of moonshine. We observed the preacher as he busted open the barrel and watched all the liquor drain into the river.

"We got enough of the good stuff to sell. We don't need that," he quipped.

We looked for push poles for over an hour, and we had almost decided it would be just as quick to make them when Cletus called out.

"I see them! I see them!"

Cletus had been about a hundred yards downstream. Sure enough, there were two poles he had found stuck in the mud about eight feet off the bank in the water. The preacher took a step into the river.

"Here, grab my hand."

I grabbed the preacher's hand and Cletus grabbed mine. He pulled the poles out of the water, passing them up to the shore, and we were soon ready to be on our way.

After the storm, the river was so calm it was almost glassy. The woods along the bank were still and quiet. We had almost forgotten the reason we were headed south. We were escaping a death sentence for murder. Two murders. Neither of which we were guilty of. Well, maybe one. But we would be blamed for both.

I had forgotten what day it was.

"How long have we been on the river?" I asked.

"It's been four days since I met up with you boys," said the preacher.

Four days? That's all? It was two days since we left Cairo before we met the preacher. Less than a week! It seemed more like a month.

I wondered if Cletus was as surprised as I was.

"Cletus, we've been gone for less than a week," I said.

"Seems like a month, Mr. Mike." *My sentiments exactly.*

Although the river appeared calm, it was moving us quickly downstream.

"We could make good time to Memphis, Mr. Mike," said Cletus, his eyes glued to the river ahead.

There was that voice again. Cletus was so different; he didn't learn good English overnight. Cletus knew it all along. He knew math. He knew much more than he had let on to. *Why was he not like this before? And why did the Reverend call him Odysseus?*

I looked at the preacher. He was flopped against the inside of the boat and already in deep sleep. Cletus was rubbing his eyes and shaking his head to stay awake. Since the storm, we had not gotten much sleep. Cletus and I did not want to stop traveling. *The more distance we had between us and the lynch mob, the better,* I thought. With that in mind, we seemed to have new vigor to push on. Only, it was becoming too dark to navigate safely for much longer. We decided to stop for the night and get an early, early start in the morning. As we prepared the fire for the evening, I thought back to Cletus and the change in his speech and his words. As soon as we had a moment, I was determined to find out what happened. *And who is Odysseus?*

CHAPTER 30

TRYING TO GET THE TRUTH ABOUT CLETUS

Blackwater had awoken by the time we had almost finished cooking two large catfish we caught near the bank.

"Smells good! I'm famished!" drooled Blackwater. He stood there watching as Cletus pulled the fish off the spit and onto a grassy spot near the fire.

"I can't wait to eat!" Blackburn said. This was same Blackwater who turned his nose up to the same meal we offered him the first time we had met.

As I reached to break off a piece for myself, Blackwater interrupted me.

"I think we should pray."

"You're right, Reverend," agreed Cletus, "The Lord has been good to us."

I watched as both of them bowed their heads.

"Dear, Lord," prayed Blackwater, "we come to You with grateful hearts that You saw fit to spare our lives through this ordeal. Thank You. Thank you that You love us and have taken care of us thus far. Thank You for giving us our mission in life and for directing our paths. Forgive me, Lord, when I have failed You as a witness. Thank you for all your blessings and for this food before us. Use it to nourish our bodies and use our bodies for Your service. In Jesus Name, Amen."

As I went back to the fish again, I heard Cletus start to pray.

"And dear Lord, I want to thank You for bringing me to this point in my life. Thank You for Reverend Blackwater who has reminded me, again, of Your greatness and of Your love toward me. Forgive me for the times I forgot to seek Your guidance. And, Lord, I thank You for Mister Mike, a true friend who has stuck by me like a brother. Bless him, Lord, and bless his family, too. In the Name of Jesus, Amen."

I peeked out to see if they would be praying anymore, but then I saw the two sit and begin breaking up the fish to eat. I joined them with a lot of questions.

"Okay, Cletus, what's going on?" I demanded.

"What do you mean, Mister Mike?" he answered.

"You know what I mean. The way you talk, your speech. You sound more like Blackwater than you do a slave. I mean, what going on?"

Blackwater jumped into the conversation. "It's an amazing story, Young Mike. I could hardly believe it myself. Your friend here is a very smart and articulate young man. I was shocked at how much he knows. The other night while you were sleeping, he told me his whole life story and it was unbelievable!" Blackwater looked at Cletus. "Go ahead, you tell it!"

Cletus grinned and looked toward me. "It's a long story, Mister Mike. Are you sure you want to know?"

"Yes!" I implored.

"Well, here it goes. It started with my grandfather, in Virginia. He was a slave too, but he was different. He was an inside slave."

"An inside slave?" I asked.

"He didn't work in the fields. He was an elegant slave who dressed in fine clothes and took care of business in the big house. You see, he worked for a plantation owner who had a son who was crippled and my grandfather had to take care of him every day."

"Okay, but how did that give you such good speech and big words?"

"The plantation owner would have visiting teachers and tutors who would come to teach that boy. Sometimes they would stay a few weeks or a month or two, and sometimes they would stay over a year at a time. Every lesson taught to that boy was a lesson to my grandfather. He learned about mathematics, history, law, Latin, Greek, mythology."

"You mean he went to school?"

"No, not school. He just was there, listening, studying in his head, and then he would go home at night and he would tell the lessons and stories he learned to his children. One was my mother. Her name was Helen. My mother loved the stories and she loved to learn. My grandfather had learned good speech and he taught my mom how to speak just like rich folk."

"He was in Virginia and you're here from New Orleans. What happened?"

"My mother was bought by a rich family from New Orleans. She was in inside slave. She had manners and she could speak well. She met my father at the French Quarter. He was unloading crates of vegetables and she had been sent to buy food. Everybody would buy and sell at the French Market. She told me it was love at first sight. They got married, but nobody knew. Then, later, I was born. My parents didn't see much of each other. He was working on the Cairo Queen for the older Mr. Morten and didn't have much time to be with my mother. When I was about twelve, my mother heard my father had drown in the Mississippi. Mr. Mills was on that ship and he was just as mean then as now. I believe he had something to do with my father's death. He didn't just fall off the ship, I believe in my heart now that Mills had something to do with my father's death too. So, what I did wasn't just for Mr. Morten, but for my father also."

There was a long pause before anyone spoke. I wasn't sure if Blackwater caught on about Mr. Morten, I needed to change the temperament before he started asking questions.

"So, everything you know was taught to you by your mother."

"Right."

"But how come you never talked like that around the boat, or when you were with me?"

"Sorry about that Mister Mike. I did slip a few times, but you never really noticed. What would have happened if I was in front of those rivermen and I walked up to them and started talking like I do now?"

"Well, maybe I can understand around those men. They were ignorant animals anyway, but around me – why around me?"

"I didn't know you very well Mister Mike. I didn't know if I could trust you yet."

"So, Cletus, that's how you came to speak so good."

"Wait!" interrupted Blackwater, "Tell him about your name!"

"You name?" I asked. "Let me guess. Cletus is not your name?"

"Well, yes and no. My real name is not Cletus. It's Odysseus."

"Odysseus? Where did you get a name like that?" I was still baffled.

Blackwater laughed out loud. "This is the good part! Tell him Cletus, or should I say, Odysseus?" Blackwater was still snickering.

"My mother gave me that name after the main character in Homer's epic poem, the *Illiad*."

"Whoa! Whoa!" My head was already too full. "Hold on a minute! Back up!" I was beginning to feel overwhelmed and very ignorant. "So, your name is Odysseus, not Cletus. So why do we call you Cletus, and not your real name?"

Cletus suddenly became pensive, and I felt I had hit a nerve.

"Once," he started, "when I was only seven years old, I was asked what my name was. I said 'Odysseus' and the man laughed at me. He asked me where I got such a fancy name for such an ugly little nig…" Odysseus paused and swallowed hard.

"I told him it was from the *Illiad*, by Homer and that it was from Greek mythology. I mentioned the Trojan horse and Greeks at war with Troy, but, before I could say any more, he accused me of trying to sass and make fun of him. And then…" Odysseus paused again, "I got my first beating at the hands of a white man." He hesitated.

"My momma and my daddy would whip me if I ever was bad or lied. This was the first time I was whipped for telling the truth."

"So, you changed your name?"

"Yes, and I decided I would not ever let anyone think I was smart or that I knew anything. It's not worth the beating like I got that day. I just picked a common name, and here I am."

There was a long pause before Blackwater spoke up.

"He's smart, Mister Mike. I know men who went to the University who can't hold a candle to Cletus, uh, I meant to say, Odysseus!" Blackwater was grinning ear to ear. "And he is a Christian. This trip almost caused me to lose my faith, but it was Odysseus who helped me see the light again and after what has happened over the last few days, I know now God still has a great plan for me and my ministry."

Blackwater almost seemed to be glowing.

I was stunned. I thought back to that night with Morten. He wanted me to teach Cletus, or Odysseus, or whatever his name was. According to Blackwater, that black boy might be the smartest person I had ever met. I was quiet for the rest of the night. Blackwater and – Odysseus – seemed to have renewed strength and sat around the fire late into the night, singing songs to each other. Cletus would sing -

Steal away, steal away, steal away to Jesus!

Steal away, steal away home, I ain't got long to stay here!

My Lord He calls me, He calls me by the thunder,

The trumpet sounds within my soul;

I ain't got long to stay here!

Green trees a-bending, Poor sinner stands a-trembling;

The trumpet sounds within my soul, I ain't got long to stay here!

Then Blackwater would sing –

Jesus, Lover of My Soul, Let me to Thy bosom fly,

While the nearer waters roll, While the tempest still is high!

Hide me, O my Savior, hide, Till the storm of life is past,

Safe into the haven guide, O receive my soul at last!

The words rang in my head all night.

31

CHAPTER

BACK TO NORMAL ON THE RIVER

The next day was just as quiet and calm as the day before the storm. As we had wanted, we started out very early. For the first time since the storm, we saw others on the river.

"The storm shut down a lot of traffic on the river, Mister Mike, but it's back alive now."

We tried not to draw much attention to ourselves as we pushed forward. As others would wave, and bid us a good day, we would wave back, friendly like, but tried to not let our faces be seen. Since they were going upstream, they might hear about the fugitives wanted for murder and report seeing us. Of course, they would not be looking for three men. *Or would they?* And those fellows chasing us would not recognize our boat or its cargo.

During the rest of the day, the number of boats increased and we would politely return every wave so as not to arouse suspicion. We needed to time our arrival into Memphis so as not to get much attention once we landed.

Our plan was to stop a few miles upstream and let the preacher bring it in. There were other faster boats and paddle wheels passing us downstream now, but with all the other traffic on the river, we were praying we weren't recognized.

"I know where we can stop. I've seen the place many times. It'll be perfect," Odysseus said. He was right. It was a small creek that entered the river and we could easily hide there until we could get the preacher into Memphis.

We had not thought of food too much, but now we were feeling hungry.

"I got just the thing," the preacher said, "Looky here."

He pried open a barrel of apples, still green and small, but it was food and we were starved.

That night we were just as quiet as the river. Odysseus seemed to be in a rather pensive mood, but I was ready to talk. Once the preacher had dozed off for the night, I opened up as I leaned toward Odysseus.

"Odysseus, I got a question for you."

"I'll try to answer it."

"Can you tell me those stories, the ones your granddaddy learned and taught your mom and she taught you?"

"Well, my favorite is the Trojan War. That happened in a city called Troy. You see, the Greeks were mad at the prince of Troy because he had come to Greece and stolen the beautiful queen, Helen. She was supposed to be the most beautiful woman there ever was."

"And your mom, isn't her name Helen?"

"Yep, my grandfather named her after the queen, because he said she was the most beautiful baby he had ever seen."

"But who is Odysseus?"

"Hold on, I'm getting to that. The Greeks had over one thousand ships, full of soldiers ready to attack Troy. But the city had walls as thick as mountains, and the whole Greek army could not penetrate the city. So, and here is the good part, Odysseus was a general in the Greek army. He had a plan to get into the city. He took wood from some of the ships and he built this great horse, as tall as any tree you had ever seen. Then he sent the ships away to the other side of the sea to hide. He then took a band of men and they hid inside the horse. Well, when the men of Troy came out, they saw the ships had gone and this massive horse was left. They thought it was a gift from the Greeks, so they brought it inside their fortress." Odysseus got real quiet, as if telling some great battle secret.

"When it became night, Odysseus and his men climbed out of the horse and opened the gate to let the Greek army in and they won the war."

"That was a quick war, wasn't it?" I interjected, trying to sound like I had a little learning.

Odysseus laughed, "No, it wasn't quick. The war took ten years from start to finish!"

I smiled at my own ignorance, but inside I realized I had a lot to learn about the world around me. Odysseus continued telling me stories about a man named Jason and how he captured a golden fleece. He told me about a man named Icarus who tried to fly to the sun with wings of feathers and wax and how he got too close to the sun and the heat melted the wax and he fell to earth and was never found.

It was late in the night before we, or really, Odysseus, stopped talking. When he did stop, a melancholy look covered his face.

Odysseus looked sadder than I ever remembered him. He looked down, with his huge shoulders hunched over his knees. He didn't seem like a slave to me. He seemed free and doing whatever he wanted. But then I realized running from the law was not a choice most folk would relish. But being a slave was probably a lot worse.

I fell asleep not feeling very free myself.

"It's her! It's her! She's coming!" I woke up to Odysseus screaming and yelling.

"Cletus, what are you yelling about?" I said, as I leaped from a groggy sleep.

"It's her, Mr. Mike! It the Cairo Queen! She's coming."

I paused to listen. "I don't hear a thing. There's nothing there."

"Yes, she is Mr. Mike and she's coming down river." Cletus ran to the edge of the bank, straining to look up stream. I followed and soon the preacher was standing behind us.

"What's all this fuss about?"

"It's my boat, preacher."

"Your boat?"

"It was the boat I was on when the captain was killed and…"

"Killed? Odysseus! Someone killed someone?"

"Mister Morten isn't dead! I can hear him!"

"Odysseus you must be dreaming. I don't hear a thing but you bellowing. That could be any paddle wheeler."

"No, it's him Mister Mike; I told you I can hear it. That's what I do best, and I can hear things. I know how he blows his whistle. He isn't dead. It's coming, and Mister Morten is alive. He wasn't killed! Maybe we didn't kill Mills!"

"Well, let's be very careful, Odysseus. Let's just be very careful and see before we give ourselves away." We continued to watch, waiting to see what would be coming around the bend. And then, there she was. Her whistle was letting off steam and the big paddle wheel was churning up the muddy Mississippi.

Odysseus and I were straining to see who was piloting the boat and who else could have been on it. Could it have been Mister Morten, come back from the dead? Or the sheriff and his posse? Or those scoundrels who had chased us on the Ohio after we ran off with their cargo?

As I peered across the deck, my eyes almost popped out of my head.

"M-m-mom?" I stuttered. *Could that be my mother?* I wasn't really sure, but it looked like her, and it looked like my brothers on either side of her! *It can't be, but maybe.* I couldn't hold back. This time I yelled it out. "Mom! Mom!" I dashed out into the water, wading deeper and deeper until Odysseus grabbed me by the collar and pulled me back.

"Are you wanting to drown or are you trying to get us caught?"

Whoever was on the boat didn't hear me, and the <u>Cairo Queen</u> kept paddling right past us. "Let's hurry and catch up with it!" I yelled.

"Right," answered Odysseus.

We both jumped in the boat, grabbing the poles to push away. We looked up and the preacher was still standing there with a shocked stare on his face.

"Someone killed someone?" he asked again, still staring, as his eyes darted back and forth between me and Odysseus.

CHAPTER 32

A Lot of Explaining to Do

Blackwater was astounded. He hadn't moved a muscle as he stood stoic on the bank. "You killed someone?"

"We thought the Captain was dead."

"You tried to kill a river boat Captain?"

"We thought he was killed and Odysseus killed the one we thought killed him, but he is alive and - ,"

"There were two men killed? I have been traveling with two wanted killers? I thought you might have been guilty of petty larceny, but not murder."

"It was self-defense."

"If we had stayed, we would have hung."

"I guess so! You killed someone!"

By now the <u>Cairo Queen</u> was headed downstream, and almost out of sight.

"Look, preacher, if we had been murderers, don't you think we would have killed you by now?"

"Well, that is a comforting thought! You may still."

"No! No! We are not killers."

"That is not how it sounds to me!"

"Look, we're headin' to catch up with that paddle wheel. Are you coming with us or not?"

"Now you are trying to steal all my wares."

"No, that's not it. We just want to catch up with that boat before it gets to New Orleans! You can have it all; we're just trying to reach that boat. Are you coming or not?"

"I guess I trusted this far. All right!" And the preacher jumped on the boat as Odysseus and I feverishly pushed us toward the paddle wheel.

It seemed the harder we pushed the father downstream the paddle wheel got.

"We are never going to catch her."

"Oh yes we will, Mr. Mike, she's going stop in Memphis and I know where she docks. We'll be there in no more than an hour."

Just like Odysseus said, we soon came up to Memphis. I had never seen anything like it. There were boats and paddlewheels as far as I could see. Piers jutted out into the river and large buildings lined the water front. I had never seen so many people running every which way.

"Can you believe this preacher?"

"This place? This is small potatoes compared to Philadelphia or New York or even Pittsborough."

"There she is. It's her! It's her!"

"Be careful, Odysseus. Let's check it out first."

Odysseus guided us to the outside of the boat and tied us securely to the rails along its side. The three of us crawled over the side and crouched low.

"What am I hiding for? I haven't done anything wrong," said the preacher as he stood straight up.

"Sh-h-h-h," we said, still crouching low as we crept along the deck.

"No! If you are as innocent as you say, you have nothing to fear. Face this like a man. God will go with you, I promise."

He jumped up and started strutting around the boat ahead of us.

"Captain! Captain! There you are. Sir, my name is Reverend Blackwater from Philadelphia, and I have the two fugitives you are seeking. I believe they are willing to surrender and face the horrible consequences. I myself believe they are innocent, but they are willing to give themselves up and face a court of law."

What is he doing? I said to myself. We were about ready to jump back into the boat and disappear, when we heard Blackwater talking again and it stunned us.

CHAPTER 33

A Surprising Reunion

We both thought this was the end of the line for us.

"What's that? Oh my! You don't mean?" We could hear the preacher, but not who he was speaking to.

"Really? That will be great news for these two young men!"

Great news? What, we were going to be shot instead of hung? Just as I was about to crawl back over the rail of the boat, I heard the voice of my mom.

"Michael?"

I froze in my tracks and slowly turned toward her. Before I could blink, she had wrapped her arms around me and was squeezing me tightly around the chest, locking my arms against the sides of my body. My two brothers had now grabbed me around the waist. I tried to talk. "Mom, I am so sorry about the Captain and about Mister Mills, we didn't mean to kill him."

"Mike, I am so glad you are alive!" My mom was now crying, then she added, "We had found the men whose raft you had."

"Mom, we didn't mean to steal the raft, but –"

"And then we found the wreckage, and I just knew you were dead."

"Mom, listen, we didn't mean to –"

Just then someone grabbed my shoulder and said, "Hello, son."

I turned, and it was the Captain, Mr. Morten.

"It is you! You are alive! We thought you were dead! I saw your body. But, you're alive!"

Odysseus was standing behind him, all grinning like and he blurted out. "Mills - he isn't dead either! I didn't kill him! He's alive too!"

"What?" I said, shocked at what I was hearing.

The Captain answered. "Mills had wounded me and would have killed me for sure, if you and Cletus had not stopped him."

"But he isn't dead?" quizzed Odysseus again.

"A few broken bones. Just enough to keep him from running away until the sheriff came."

"Is he in jail?" asked Odysseus.

"Yes, waiting for your friend here to testify," Mr. Morten said and motioned toward me. All eyes here soon on me.

"Beg your pardon?"

"Right now it is his word against mine about killing my father. You heard what he said, didn't you?"

"About killing your father? Yes, we heard him confess it."

"But what about the two men who were chasing us and the boat we stole with the liquor and what about the ones who were trying to track us down?"

"The two men you tossed in the water were wanted criminals. They stole the liquor from the federal government who had confiscated it from an illegal moonshiner in Pittsborough. They tried to convince the authorities that you had done it, but the wanted posters the sheriff received told us otherwise. And the men who were tracking you down were only trying to find you to come back and testify in Mills' trial."

I breathed a sigh of relief and then I turned to my mom.

"But, Mom, why are you here?"

"Right before you disappeared, the Captain had asked me to marry him, and after everything had happened, he offered to help me find you. Then we saw your boat wrecked on the bank after that storm, and I thought you were dea-," she stopped and started to cry.

"Wow!" I should have known something was happening between my mom and Mr. Morten. He had often stopped by my house for visits, which I thought was just to buy vegetables, but now I remembered the many times he had asked about her. I realized the woman Morten and Mills were arguing over was my mom.

"What happens now?" I asked

"If you are willing to testify...."

"He will," Odysseus answered for me.

"Then we'll head back to Cairo and you will testify against Mills when he stands trial for murdering my father and attempted murder of me."

"And my father?" asked Odysseus.

"I don't know, son," answered Morten, "I can believe now that Mills may have been the cause of your father's death. It may come up at Mills' trial. Either way, he will be in prison for a long time for what he did."

"And after the trial?" I asked

"I'm hoping your mom will say yes," Morten said as he looked at my mom.

I turned to my mom. "Well, Mom?" I asked.

"Are you all right with that?" my mom asked.

"Sure," I said, trying not to appear that concerned, "but then what?"

"I want all of you to travel with me to New Orleans."

"New Orleans?" Odysseus said as his ears perked up, "Am I going home?"

The Captain turned to Odysseus.

"You almost lost your life trying to save mine. I don't think I could ever really repay you. But I have decided that I am going to set you free, Cletus, and then I want you to work for me - as my foreman. Will you work for me, not as a slave, but as a free man?"

"Free? Free? As your foreman? Yes, sir, I would be mighty grateful."

"And you Mike, would you still be willing to teach Cletus to read and write?"

"Well, first, his name is not Cletus. It's Odysseus."

The Captain looked puzzled.

"We'll explain it later, but to tell you the truth, Odysseus has more schooling than I could ever teach him. When you got time, ask him about the Trojan horse and the war, about the *Illiad*, and, and, about Greek met-metho-, well, whatever that word is. It's not him who needs it. I think it's me who needs to go to school."

"Well, I am very glad to hear you say that, because I want to send you and your brothers to the finest schools in New Orleans."

There was an awkward pause when no one knew what to say. Finally, Reverend Blackwater spoke up. "Praise God! Thank You Lord! I knew these boys were innocent and I was ready to stand by their side. I guess I will bid you all a fond farewell. This is where I will be starting my ministry, and with the help of these two, I will be able to start several churches here in the west."

Then Blackwater turned to the Captain and said, "Sir, I thank God you are alive," he grabbed Odysseus by the shoulders and said to the Captain, "This young man will be a fine and loyal employee, I know. He is God-fearing and as brave and honest as they come."

He then turned to my mother. "Ma'am you have a wonderful son. I believe God is going to bless him in a mighty way. You will see."

Then he took my hand and said to me, "Mr. Fink, God has His hand on you. You listen to His call and you will be very blessed." With that, Blackwater waved goodbye and climbed down to his skiff, now quite capable and skilled to manage it all by himself.

"Well, foreman Cletus, I mean, Odysseus," blurted Morten, "let's get this paddlewheel turned around and headed back to Cairo."

"Yes, sir, Captain Morten," said Odysseus, grinning ear to ear. As he turned toward the pilot house, he said to me, "Well, Mike," he paused, "I guess this is the answer to my question, 'Does the river ever end?'" Beaming, he added, "Yes it does."

www.ingramcontent.com/pod-product-compliance
Lightning Source LLC
Chambersburg PA
CBHW051345020726
47501CB00007B/2274